"You're flirting with me," Brian said

Janet didn't know whether to be pleased or angry. She started to speak, then drew back and collected her thoughts. She put her food down and firmed her chin.

He prepared himself for her reaction.

"Okay, you want to be straight with each other?"

Not necessarily. He just wanted her to understand—

"I'm attracted to you," she said, interrupting his conversation with himself. "You're kind, smart, funny and comfortingly sane…when you're not being weird about embarrassing the family."

"But you're a poor judge of character, remember?" he said brutally. "You were left at the altar—"

"Would you do that to me?" she asked ingenuously.

"No, I wouldn't, because you'd never get me anywhere near an altar."

She took another clam and studied it, then looked up at him.

"Are you a betting man?"

Dear Reader,

With this fourth book in THE ABBOTTS series, the family has become very real to me. I've explored their minds and hearts and know them as well as I know my own family. I fully expect to round a corner in Astoria and bump into the whole crowd, vacationing here for the Lewis and Clark Bicentennial.

While they're here, I'd love to be in Losthampton, sunning on the deck at Shepherd's Knoll, or having coffee on the porch at Brian's General Store and Boat Rental. Join me there one last time to witness the solution to the mystery of Abby's kidnapping, and to be on hand as Brian discovers love at last.

Best wishes,

Muriel

P.O. Box 1168
Astoria, Oregon 97103

HIS THE ABBOTTS WEDDING

Muriel Jensen

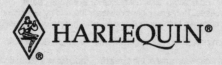

HARLEQUIN®

TORONTO • NEW YORK • LONDON
AMSTERDAM • PARIS • SYDNEY • HAMBURG
STOCKHOLM • ATHENS • TOKYO • MILAN • MADRID
PRAGUE • WARSAW • BUDAPEST • AUCKLAND

ISBN 0-373-75088-9

HIS WEDDING

Copyright © 2005 by Muriel Jensen.

All rights reserved. Except for use in any review, the reproduction or utilization of this work in whole or in part in any form by any electronic, mechanical or other means, now known or hereafter invented, including xerography, photocopying and recording, or in any information storage or retrieval system, is forbidden without the written permission of the publisher, Harlequin Enterprises Limited, 225 Duncan Mill Road, Don Mills, Ontario M3B 3K9, Canada.

All characters in this book have no existence outside the imagination of the author and have no relation whatsoever to anyone bearing the same name or names. They are not even distantly inspired by any individual known or unknown to the author, and all incidents are pure invention.

This edition published by arrangement with Harlequin Books S.A.

® and TM are trademarks of the publisher. Trademarks indicated with ® are registered in the United States Patent and Trademark Office, the Canadian Trade Marks Office and in other countries.

www.eHarlequin.com

Printed in U.S.A.

To the gang at Jarvis, Redwine and Chaloux:
Steven, Mark, Alice, Toni, Trish and Walt.
Thank you for the pleasure of your company.
Work shouldn't be this much fun.

Books by Muriel Jensen

HARLEQUIN AMERICAN ROMANCE

* Millionaire, Montana
** The Abbotts

Chapter One

"He'll listen to you. You're the one who should talk Brian into being Campbell's best man," Killian cajoled.

Janet Grant Abbott was sitting across from her brother Killian at the breakfast table on the deck off their family mansion, the August-morning breeze fluttering the linen tablecloth. Their brothers, Sawyer and Campbell, sat at opposite ends. All the women in the house were sleeping in after a family party celebrating Janet's permanent move to Losthampton had continued to the wee hours. Janet, though, had just rediscovered her brothers after a lifetime apart from them and was still fascinated that they had one another. She'd heard them talk last night about having breakfast together and had gotten up to join them.

As the eldest Abbott son, Killian was CEO of Abbott Mills, a conglomerate of corporations encompassing the production, manufacture and sale of their and other designs. He'd also acquired several unrelated holdings in an experimental foray into other areas.

Janet looked from one brother to another in confusion. "Why should Brian have to be talked into it? He's our brother…sort of."

Campbell, the youngest of the three men, shook his head. "I like to think of him that way, but technically, he's not. He's their half brother," he said, pointing to Killian and Sawyer, "but no real relation to you and me."

There *was* a visible difference in the coloring of the Abbott progeny. Killian and Sawyer were fair haired and blue eyed, an inheritance from their mother's Scottish heritage. Campbell and Janet had their French mother's dark hair and eyes. Otherwise, they had emotional characteristics in common, and a stubbornness that marked all four.

"Well, sure. *Technically*," she allowed. "But I've noticed that doesn't seem to matter around here. And he's your good friend, anyway. That should…"

Campbell was already shaking his head. He was responsible for managing the estate and the apple orchard, and was as quarrelsome as he could be charming. "I asked him while you and China were in L.A., and he made some excuse about this being the busiest time at the store and he had to be there because he was getting estimates to add on a coffee shop, or something. But I don't think that's really it."

Sawyer pushed away his empty plate. "We've invited him into the family, but apparently, he prefers to stay carefully on the fringe. Maybe he's afraid of intruding." Sawyer headed the Abbott Mills Foundation, the philanthropic arm of the family's many holdings. He was a daredevil by nature and conducted every phase of his life like an extreme sport. At thirty-five, he was four years older than Campbell and two years younger than Killian.

Janet had come to adore her brothers in the five weeks since she'd rediscovered them, but she did not want to have to talk Brian Girard into anything. She found him interesting and attractive, but he seemed to have little use for her. It was embarrassing.

They saw each other at family get-togethers, and while she managed to be polite, there was always a certain testiness to his behavior that had started the day she'd first arrived at Shepherd's Knoll, looking for China. She had accidentally run him over with a Vespa, though she'd apologized for that.

"Why can't Mom talk to him?" she'd asked with a pleading look around the table. "She and Brian are crazy about each other."

"She stays out of disagreements among her children." Killian smilingly shot down that suggestion. "If he really were her son, maybe she could bully him into doing it. But she can't. It's up to you, Janby. We're counting on you to make him change his mind."

He *would* have to call her Janby. It was what the family had created out of Janet, the name her adopted family had given her, and Abby, the name given her at birth. For the first few days after the DNA test had proven she was the Abbotts' daughter, kidnapped from her bedroom at fourteen months, everyone had stumbled over her name. She'd arrived as Janet Grant, but she'd become Abigail Abbott. The composite name charmed her.

"He likes to talk to you," Sawyer added.

"No, he doesn't," she denied. "It only seems that way to you because you can't hear what we're talking about. Usually, we're disagreeing about something, or he's pointing out my mistakes. He doesn't like me."

And that was the real source of their antagonism—at least, on her part. She liked Brian, had been attracted to him from the first time she'd seen him. Unfortunately, that was after she'd run him over with the Vespa.

She'd hoped that had been the cause of his antagonism and that he'd get over it. But they'd been in each other's company half-a-dozen times since then, at one family function or another, and he showed absolutely no interest in her except to take the opposite position on whatever she talked about, or to illustrate how wrong she was about everything whenever he could.

"That's ridiculous," Campbell said, disputing her. "Everyone likes you."

"Come on," Killian coaxed. "Cordie and I are standing up for Sawyer and Sophie. If you and Brian are witnesses for Campbell and China, it'll be the perfect family thing. And though Mom's staying out of it, we know she'd love it, too. Help us do this."

Even Janet knew she was defeated. Killian, Sawyer and Campbell were the world's most perfect brothers. They'd welcomed her home, done everything they could to make her comfortable, protected her from the press, explained to her with the clinical detachment of people accustomed to wealth that Killian had opened various bank accounts in her name—checking, savings, a healthy IRA, a trust fund, all of which amounted to a sum so staggering to the simple woman she'd been so far that she'd been unable to speak. And their father had put a block of Abbott Mills stock in her name when she was born, as he'd done for each of her brothers. Killian had added to it over the years as he'd added to their own—in faith that she'd be returned to them one day.

And here she was. She loved them for their faith, not their wealth, and she didn't see that she could deny them anything.

"Fine," she said, afraid she might fail but determined to try. "I'll see what I can do."

She made her way to the estate's vast garage and climbed astride the Vespa, determined to get Brian into a tuxedo for the wedding—whatever it took. As she sped down the lane and up the road that bordered the orchard, leaving the fanciful yellow Victorian mansion behind, the air was sweet with the promise of apples and tangy with the ever-present bite of the salty ocean that encompassed Long Island, New York, on this late-summer morning.

The sun warm on her back, she turned onto the road that led to Brian's General Store and Boat Rental, knowing he'd be open, since it was almost nine o'clock. She enjoyed the smooth ride, going over in her mind various ways to approach Brian about taking part in the wedding.

She considered making an effort to charm him, but she usually did that and he failed to notice.

She could attempt to approach him with subtlety, but he was a very direct man and probably wouldn't even get the point.

Heaping guilt on him seemed like her only option when she caught sight of a battered blue Trans Am turning off a side road and falling in line behind her. She recognized the car immediately. Souped-up and poorly kept, it belonged to Buzz Merriman, reporter-photographer for the *Meteor,* a tabloid determined to make something unsavory out of her return to Losthampton.

Killian had explained to her that the Abbott policy toward the press was to treat them respectfully without revealing family secrets. He insisted the reporters were just doing their jobs and could be useful to the foundation's efforts if the family had their goodwill.

That might work with the reporter from the *Losthampton Leader,* with the one who'd been sent from the *New York Mirror* and the many radio and television reporters who'd been following her since she'd first come to Shepherd's Knoll five weeks ago. But she was sure that didn't hold for Merriman. For one thing, he had no goodwill to cultivate. His stories on Janet always focused on where she'd been and what she'd done in the least flattering way possible rather than on the facts behind her restoration to the family.

His last piece suggested that she and China, though raised by an adoptive family as sisters, would now be at odds because Janet had been discovered to be little Abigail returned when everyone had first thought China was the long-missing heiress. China's engagement to Campbell, the reporter wrote, was a creative way for China to get the Abbott name.

Janet might have forgiven him for hurting her, but causing her sister pain was unpardonable.

If the Vespa had been any match for the Trans Am, she'd have done a quick turn and taken Merriman on in a game of chicken then and there, but she saw evasion as the wiser move.

She sped down another side road, knowing that the narrow strip ended at the high bank of sand at the back of a waterfront inn, and was pleased to see him follow. Just before the expanse of beach, she took a left through a thin grove of trees. The Vespa swerved in and out of the spindly trunks as she heard the Trans Am's brakes screechingly applied.

She chanced a glance over her shoulder just to see the car rock from the force of Merriman's abrupt stop. She enjoyed her success a moment too long, though, and turned back in time to get a pine bough in the face, a pine cone down her shirt and a vicious bump to her backside as she rode over the exposed roots of several trees.

She braked breathlessly at the edge of the grove, the back of Brian's shop visible just ahead of her. It was a beautiful scene, with the rustic little shop in the foreground, a pier jutting out into the water, all his small rental boats tied to it.

But she wasn't in the mood to enjoy it. This was a fool's errand and she was arriving to fulfill it in a bad mood from evading Buzz and taking a beating on her ride through the woods.

She caught sight of Brian, tall and loose limbed, striding along the pier, his blond hair catching the sun.

There was a natural arrogance in his bearing that was both appealing and annoying. She just didn't understand him.

She decided that if charm and subtlety were out in dealing with him, attitude would have to do.

BRIAN SAT on the top step on the porch at the front of his shop, drinking a cup of coffee while reading the *Losthampton Leader.* He growled to himself over the front-page article about Janet's move to Losthampton.

Long-lost Heiress Home Again, the caption read under a photo of Janet that must have been taken on her return from Los Angeles two days ago, after she and China had gone back to close up their apartments and make the permanent move to Shepherd's Knoll.

From the small plane visible some distance behind her, the setting was obviously the airport. Her hair was short and fluffy, her bright eyes squinting against the sun. Her face claimed most of the frame; China was relegated to one small corner of the shot.

At a glance, she looked like any other young woman on a casual afternoon. It was the second look that made the reader realize she was someone special. Then her good breeding showed in the tilt of her head and the set of her shoulders. The wit and intellect in her eyes exalted a simple prettiness to fascinating beauty, and the strength in the line of her mouth made one want to root for her without even knowing if she needed support.

The article revealed all the known details of her kidnap, the family's position in the world of business, her brothers' accomplishments, then her own history as a successful stockbroker. She was quoted as saying she hadn't known where her interest in business and the stockmarket had come from in a family of cheerful, middle-class Americans who never had anything to invest, until she discovered she was an Abbott.

He read with interest one of her friends' remarks about Janet's broken engagement three years earlier to a minor-league rock star, a month before the wedding.

It went on to reveal that her adopted sister had come to Losthampton—thinking she might be the missing Abigail, but that a DNA test had proved she wasn't. And that had brought Janet onto the scene.

He was just about to give the reporter credit for a job not too badly done, when he got to the part about himself:

"Brian Girard, the illegitimate son of Susannah Stewart Abbott, Nathan Abbott's first wife and mother of the two oldest Abbott sons, and Corbin Girard, the Abbotts' neighbor and longtime business rival, has been welcomed into the bosom of the family." It continued in praise of the family's generosity, considering that Corbin Girard was responsible for setting a fire to their home and vandalizing Brian's business. It explained in detail that Brian had been legally disowned for defecting to the Abbott camp by giving them information that stopped them from making a business deal they would have regretted. He had no idea how they'd gotten that information, unless one of the family had told them.

Brian threw the paper into the trash and strode, coffee cup in hand, down his dock. The two dozen boats he'd worked so hard to repair and refresh bobbed at the ends of their lines, a testament to his determination to start over at something he enjoyed.

The repainted and refinished shop was stocked with the old standbys people came in for day after day, as well as a few new gourmet products, a line of sophisticated souvenirs, and shirts and hats with his logo on them—a rowboat with a grocery bag in the bow, visible proof of his spirit to survive in the face of his father's continued hatred.

He could fight all the roadblocks in his path, he thought, looking out at the sun rising to embroider the water with light, but how could he fight the truth? No matter what he did, he would always be the son of a woman who'd thrown away her husband and her two other sons like outdated material, and of a man who'd rejected him since the day he was born and who had no concept of purpose but to make more money than the next man and prevent him from catching up by whatever means it took.

The sorry fact was that Brian couldn't fight it. He could do his best to be honest and honorable, but that would never inspire a newspaper article. Every time his name came up, it would be as the son of his reprehensible parents.

He didn't know what to do about it.

"You're an idiot," he told himself firmly, "if you allow yourself to be hurt by what you can't change and by what you had no control over in the first place."

Right. He got that part. But what about all the other

people connected to him—like the Abbotts—who would have to hear or listen to the old scandal dragged up again as the true meat of the story whenever they did something newsworthy?

He'd been giving that a lot of thought and hoping for a solution other than the obvious: move out of their light. He was a smart man; it would come to him.

Meanwhile, the brief lull between his early-rising customers and the late-stirring sack rats would be over soon and he had things to do. As he walked along the dock, checking his little fleet, he noticed a loose knot on the line securing a square-stern canoe. He'd just gotten down to tighten it when a movement to his left made him turn. Janet was standing nearby, in a white shirt knotted at her waist and white shorts. She smelled of something floral that permeated even the smell of salt water and diesel. She was slightly disheveled, and that seemed at odds with the royal bearing of her squared shoulders.

He caught a glimpse of tanned and shapely limbs before he concentrated on making sure the line was fast.

"Good morning," he said.

"Hi," she replied in a purposeful tone. "Do you have a few minutes to talk?"

Finally certain the line was secure, he straightened and saw uncharacteristic confusion in her eyes, backed by a small spark of anger.

"Yes, I do." He put his hands in the pockets of his khaki shorts, wondering what was going on. "What do you want to talk about?"

She studied him a moment, as though reluctant to bring up whatever she'd come to discuss. Then she made an impatient gesture with one hand that widened the space between the bottom of her shirt and the top of her shorts, distracting him again.

"My sister's wedding," she finally blurted.

Oh, no. She was an emissary from Campbell. Or China. He refocused on her face.

"You're here to talk me into being best man," he guessed, starting back toward the shop.

She fell into step beside him. "Yes. I know your decision is none of my business, but Campbell and China are very disappointed, and that *is* my concern. You have to reconsider."

"Campbell has dozens of friends."

"He wants you."

Yeah. Brian liked him, too, but here was that ugly truth again that would only darken an otherwise beautiful day.

"Did you see yourself in the paper this morning?" he asked, taking her arm to steer her around a forgotten bait bucket as she watched a seagull soar overhead.

"Thank you. No. Why? What did it say?" She gently disengaged her arm and said grimly, "I doubt the readership finds me as interesting as all those overeager reporters think I am."

Brian took issue with that. "I'm sure the locals find you very interesting. Many of them remember when you were kidnapped, and they grieved with your family. Everyone around here loves the Abbotts. And here you are, back in their lives, beautiful and smart. They consider it's good justice that you're home again."

"Good justice," she repeated. They'd reached the store and she stopped to lean an arm on the newel post. "I do know I'm very lucky. But that's not the same as being special. I'm thrilled to be home among such wonderful people, but I hate this living-in-a-fishbowl stuff. That tabloid reporter from the *Meteor* even followed me here this morning! I'm sure the front page of the next issue will have a photo of the back of me on the Vespa, with the headline Heiress Runs Away."

Brian couldn't imagine what would be bad about a photo of the back of her—whatever the headline. His guess was that her good looks and lively personality were going to keep her in the public eye for a long time.

"So…I'm sorry, I got distracted by my dislike of press coverage," she said. "Did you have a point to make about the article?"

"Yes." He leaned an elbow on the opposite post. "It talked about your broken engagement a month before your wedding, and I was mentioned in the ending paragraphs. Happy news always seems to require dredging up every bad moment in the past."

"True." She shrugged philosophically. She wasn't getting the point.

"Well, the press will surely give the Abbotts' double wedding front-page coverage. All that happy news. "'The grooms were handsome,'" he pretended to quote, "'the brides were radiant, the mother-of-the-grooms was so happy to have her daughter back serving as her brother and adopted sister's maid of honor,' yada yada. If I'm best man, it'll end with 'Brian Girard, best man, is the son of the first Mrs. Abbott, who ran off with the chauffeur after being impregnated by the neighbor and Nathan Abbott's arch ene—'"

"I know, I know." She nodded to cut him off.

"Then you can see why I don't want to do that to them."

"Forgive me," she said, "but I can't. That'll probably end the story whether you're at the wedding or not. And your refusal to be with them hurts them far more than any old sticks-and-stones reporting ever would."

"Easy for you to say," he argued. "It's not your wedding."

That accusation seemed to inflate her bad mood. "It's my sister's wedding. And it's as important to me as mine would be. You said they brought up *my* broken engagement and the very newsworthy way it happened. Well, you don't see *me* going into a decline over it."

"Whoa!" He got a little indignant himself. "I'd hardly describe my reaction as a decline. And you've been cranky since you got here, over the photographer who followed you. So don't go casting aspersions on me. My reasons for wanting to stay away are in consideration of the Abbotts!"

"Well, they want you there," she said, then started off toward the Vespa she'd run him over with when she'd first arrived in Losthampton. It leaned against the No Vehicles Allowed sign. She stopped to turn to him and add, "At this point, I have little purpose at Shepherd's Knoll but to try to contribute to the well-being of my family, who suffered so much while I was gone. And considering the way they've welcomed you into the bosom of the family, I'd think you'd feel the same. So I'm going to tell them you've changed your mind, and that you'll be happy to be best man." With a toss of her head, she strode off toward the bike.

He hurried to intercept her. "You may be able to order people around in L.A., Miss Grant Abbott, but this is my place. You don't dictate what happens here."

"We're talking about my only sister's wedding," she retorted, yanking back out of his reach. "And you're not going to…aagh!"

Whatever he was not going to do was drowned in salt water when she fell backward into the inlet.

Chapter Two

Her and her big mouth. The shriek Janet had been in the middle of when she felt herself falling had caused her to swallow water. As she sank into the cold Atlantic, she felt as though she'd also ingested one of the small boats—or at least, an oar.

The moment she got over the shock of her fall, she struggled upward, choking. She collided with the bottom of a boat and pulled herself around it, spotting sunlight. The light disappeared when the next boat bobbed against the first one. She groped her way back as she spotted sunlight in that direction. Her lungs were bursting as the shaft of sunlight disappeared again when the first boat now swung the other way.

Resisting panic, she followed it to its stern, but it drifted out with her to the end of its line.

Panic fought back. Had all this turmoil in her life, all this discovery, been intended simply to bring her to this point where she would…die?

It didn't seem possible, and yet here she was, unable to find the surface, unable to—

Something grabbed the back of her shirt and she was thrust upward until her head and shoulders cleared the surface. She gasped for air, choking painfully, spewing water.

A hand swiped her clinging hair out of her face. "Janet? Are you all right?" Brian asked.

She tried to open her eyes, but all she could do was cough.

Brian swam a small distance, his arm hooked around her middle, taking her with him. Then he put one of her hands on something solid, his legs tucked under her like the seat of a chair to keep her in place.

"You have a hold of the ladder," he said, placing her other hand beside the first. Just two rungs and you'll be sitting on the pier. Come on. Up."

She couldn't coordinate the movement, then his hand, under her backside, pushed her up. Her feet found an underwater rung and she propelled herself over the top. She was on her hands and knees and beginning to drag in air.

Brian swung up beside her, putting a hand to her back as he squatted to look into her face. "Janet?"

"Yes." She was embarrassed, but somehow her annoyance with him had fled. Nothing like immersion in cold water to stabilize a mood. "Yes, I'm still Janet. Did you think I couldn't come up because I was having my name changed?"

He barked a laugh. "Your sense of humor has survived." Then he lifted her up into his arms. "I've got a shower in the back of the shop."

She held on to his neck as he strode up the steps. "I couldn't find my way between the boats," she said, unable to believe that had been so difficult. "Every time I went for the sunlight, the boats bumped together again."

"My fault," he replied, walking through the shop and into a small area in the rear. "I was pushing them apart, looking for you from the pier, so when your opening disappeared, it was probably me, shoving from the other side."

"Nice guy."

"What do you want from the son of Susannah Abbott and Corbin Gir—"

She put a hand over his mouth. "If you bring that up again," she threatened, "I'll have to bite your ear." Her position in his arms made his ear an easy target.

He stopped in front of a half-open door. She glimpsed a shower stall and a medicine cabinet, but what really caught her attention were the lively depths of Brian's blue eyes a mere inch from hers. Usually, they were so steady on her that they made her feel defensive. But today they made her feel…odd?

"And that would discourage me?" he asked with a half smile.

Her mouth fell open. Was he more interested in her than it appeared?

Before she could analyze that, he set her on her feet in the doorway and pointed to a small wicker rack of towels. "There're soap and shampoo in the shower."

"And…you can dry my clothes?"

"No, but I can give you something to change into.

I've got matching T-shirts and shorts with the store name on them. Pink, green or yellow?"

"Yellow."

He studied her. "Small? Medium?"

She folded her arms to hide a little shudder of that same sensation. "Medium."

"I'll leave them on the doorknob."

"Thank you."

She stepped into the bathroom, locked the door behind her and took the first good breath she'd had since he'd looked into her eyes and suggested that he wouldn't mind if she bit his ear.

The bathroom was small and utilitarian, all in white tile with the same checkered curtains the shop windows sported.

She peeled off her wet things and climbed into the cubicle. The showerhead was powerful, with a pulsing adjustment that went a long way toward relaxing the tense muscles in her neck and back.

He had shampoo but no conditioner. And no blow-dryer. Her hair would dry flat, but at least it would be clean.

She stepped out of the shower, wrapped a towel around her head and opened the door just enough to see if he'd placed the shorts and T-shirt on the doorknob. He had.

She grabbed them and locked the door again. She noticed in pleased surprise that he'd thought to include a three-pack of panties and a sports bra. Remarkably, everything fit. The shorts were a classic boy cut, with his logo on a hip pocket. The T-shirt had the logo across the chest.

She was staring in the mirror at her alarmingly natural face, free of makeup, and her wet hair, into which she'd tried to fluff a little volume, when there was a knock on the door.

She opened it.

Brian stood there, a pair of floral flip-flops in one hand and simple white tennies in the other. He held them up for her to make a decision.

"Ah. Perfect." She chose the tennies.

"Come out when you're ready," he said. "I've poured you a cup of coffee."

She had already slipped on the shoes and took only a moment to fluff her hair again, then concluded any effort to look fashionable was hopeless.

She found Brian tearing at a package of oatmeal cookies. He'd pulled open the curtain between the front and the back of the store, probably so that he could watch for customers.

A battered coffee table next to an old red sofa held two diner-style mugs of coffee and an empty plate. He dumped the open pack of cookies unceremoniously onto the plate.

"Good thing about owning a general store," he said, gesturing her to sit down. "You can entertain at a moment's notice."

She sank onto a sofa cushion. "And provide clothing for people who fall into the drink." She grinned in self-deprecation. "Certainly was a conversation stopper, wasn't it?"

"Yes, it was. But it doesn't have to be the end of the argument if you have more to say." He sat beside her and thought back. "As I recall, you said, 'We're talking about my sister's wedding and you're not going to—' And then you screamed."

She took a cookie, dunked it in her coffee and popped it into her mouth. "Actually, now that I've been immersed in cold water, I see your arguments more clearly."

"Really. You agree with me?"

"No," she denied firmly, "but your feelings aren't that different from mine."

He leaned back into his corner of the sofa, his legs stretched out and crossed under the table. He sipped at his coffee and waited for her to explain.

She turned toward him, cookie in one hand, cup in the other. "I'm afraid of embarrassing them, too, though for different reasons. I feel very much out of my element amid all their style and elegance. I mean, Chloe would probably never dunk a cookie in her coffee, would she?"

"Uh…I can't say I've ever seen her do it."

"See? And she's not only stylish and elegant, she's European. I am so not going to measure up to the rest of the Abbotts."

As she made that claim, an idea formed, full-blown. Three years ago, she'd been left at the altar—well, not the altar, the travel agency. Her fiancé was supposed to meet her there to pay for their honeymoon tickets to Hawaii. When he never came, she went home, to find a voice-mail message that he'd changed his mind about the wedding and was off to London.

She'd been more careful of men since then but hadn't stopped looking for the right one. And despite Brian's resistance, she was beginning to wonder if it was him. Now she thought she had a way to spend time with him to determine if he was or not. Convincing him of that, of course, would take time and effort and was a job for later.

"You're not going to measure up?" he said in disbelief. "That's ridiculous. You always behave as though—"

She interrupted with a swipe of her cookie in the air. "It's an act. I'm just afraid that one day I'm going to do something embarrassing to them."

"Get a grip, Janet," he said. "They're not royalty. They're just wealthy people who are socially well connected."

She gave him a dry look. "If I may quote you, 'Easy for you to say.' You grew up in their world. Your parents had the same standard of living, the same social connections. You know how to behave among all this—" She raised a finger to stop him when he would have interrupted her. "Yes, you have that *scandalous* background." She enunciated the word with a dramatic waggle of her eyebrows. "But people deal so much more on perception than they do fact. All people notice is that you behave like a gentleman, that you're well-spoken and well educated. Columbia, wasn't it?"

"Yes. I went to Columbia."

"I went to Las Manzanas Community College and Columbia *River* College."

"Doesn't education depend on the thirst for knowledge in the student, rather than on where he goes to school?"

"I don't imagine my brothers' Ivy League educated friends would believe that."

He studied her with a frown. "I think you have some reverse snobbery at work here."

She smiled innocently. "Why? You're convinced everyone's going to judge the Abbotts by the unfortunate circumstances of *your* birth."

He continued to frown, and she couldn't decide if he was out of arguments or out of patience. She considered it a good time to make her point.

"I've been asked to be Campbell and China's maid of honor," she said, sipping her coffee, "and I don't have the luxury of refusing them. China's my only sister and I'm hers." She paused on the chance he wanted to comment. He didn't.

"So friends and family are coming from far and wide to this wedding of the year, and I have to be part of the party and take my chances that I won't do or say something inappropriate among all those people and with all the press bound to be there. Word is the *New York Times* is sending someone."

She bit into her cookie, avoiding his eyes. Was she overdoing it? She couldn't tell. And for a usually straightforward man, he was a master at hiding what he was thinking when he wanted to.

She ate the last bite of her cookie, chewed and swallowed, buying time.

"But if you were best man," she added, putting her cup down and dusting off her hands, "I'd feel less intimidated. You can help me during the Mass. I wasn't raised Catholic and I'm not familiar with the ritual, but you are, right?"

"My mother took me to church when I was a child,

but I haven't been in a long time. I don't think your brothers have, either."

"At least you have some experience. I won't know whether to stand or sit or kneel, but you'll be beside me. You can give me a high sign. You can provide moral support during the reception, and I can deflect the reporters away from you. We'll help each other."

HER ARGUMENTS WERE very transparent. The Mass could be confusing to the uninitiated, and it was true that the congregation sat behind the wedding party, so it wasn't possible to follow their lead in sitting, standing, kneeling unless you turned around to see what they were doing—and that would be just the faux pas she seemed so worried about.

But Sophie, Sawyer's fiancée, knew the ritual; she sang in the choir at St. Paul's. Following her lead would be easy enough.

And he couldn't remember ever seeing Janet make a misstep despite her insistence that Abbott society was unfamiliar to her.

He could only deduce that she was laying it on a little thick because she was determined that her sister and her brother have the wedding they wanted, and that included him.

And, though he disliked admitting this to himself, he found it hard to refuse the appeal in her wide brown eyes. Even knowing it was as much performance as sincere emotion, he was going to let it reel him in. Undoubtedly, he would hate himself for this later.

"All right," he said.

She blinked at him. "You mean…you'll do it?"

"Yes."

"But…why?"

"Because you're so persuasive." *And,* he added silently to himself, *I'm a self-indulgent idiot.*

He rested one hand on his knee and she closed both hers over it as she beamed at him. "Thank you, Brian." Her gratitude did sound heartfelt, and her hands on his knee, even over his hand, had a very pleasant effect on his body. "They'll be so happy."

"Well, that's what we want."

The bell rang over the front door. "Excuse me," he said, getting to his feet. "Customer."

Another came in before he was finished with the first, and before he knew it, the place was suddenly hopping.

When he turned to see if everyone had been helped, he found Janet trying to reach something on a top shelf for an older woman who watched her in concern. Brian recognized the woman as a three-or-four-times-a-week customer for most of August and September.

Janet's body was stretched to its utmost, her heels off the floor, her calves and her bottom in the shorts tight with her effort. He could have watched her in that pose for a while, but he hurried to lend a hand.

"What are you after, Mrs. Lindell?" he asked.

She pointed to the back of the shelf. "That bottle of hair gel."

He caught it off the shelf and handed it to Janet. She

gave it to the woman, who already had a helmet of hair that looked as though it wouldn't move in a class five hurricane. It was carved into a curled and flipped style he remembered his mother wearing twenty-five years ago.

"Is that the right brand?" Janet asked helpfully.

"That's it exactly!" The woman gave Janet a ten-dollar bill. "I was sure you were out of it! You wouldn't believe what a sailboat can do to a hairdo." To Brian she said, "I'm glad to see you've gotten yourself another assistant. She's more attentive than that boy you just hired. The last time I was here, he was so engrossed in an argument he was having with a girl he didn't even notice me."

"I'm sorry." That was unwelcome news. Joe Fanelli was young, but he'd been so eager for the job. Part of the reason Brian had hired him was that his grandfather owned and operated Fulio's, the best restaurant in Losthampton, known for its attention to detail and customer service. Joe had worked for him after school and during summers, and Brian was sure Fulio insisted on a work ethic at least as strong as his own.

Janet passed him the ten and the three of them went to the cash register. He made the woman change and put her purchase in a bag. "Thank you for telling me," he said. "I promise that won't happen to you again."

"Thank *you.*" She took her change and chatted on about the dearth of cheerful and dependable retail help while she opened her wallet, dropped the change into the right compartment, then closed it and moved several things around in her purse so that she could put the wallet back in.

Then she picked up the bag and patted Janet's cheek with her free hand. "You'll go far, sweetie. The consumer likes a convenient place to shop and a helpful staff. My husband owns four delicatessens. I know what I'm talking about."

She winked at Brian. "Bye, now."

Brian watched her walk away, hoping he wouldn't have to fire Joe Fanelli.

"I think I know what Joe's problem is," Janet said, leaning a hip against his counter.

That surprised him. "I wasn't aware you knew him?"

"I don't. But I heard the ladies at the beauty shop talking about him when I had my hair trimmed just before I left for L.A."

"And?"

"And," she said gravely, "his girlfriend is pregnant. That's why he's put off college for a year. Her parents are furious at both of them. His parents are angry at him. Even the girlfriend wants him to go to school. She's insisting she'll get a job and raise the baby and wait for him to graduate. He wants to get married and assume his responsibilities."

Brian leaned against the other side of the register. "You ladies really discuss things in depth over hair trimmings."

"Having your hair or your nails done inspires confidences. It's a fact." She looked worried. "Are you going to fire him? He needs the job."

"I understand that. But I'd like to stay in business, and that won't happen with customers being ignored. I'll talk to him. Then if he doesn't shape up, I'll fire him."

She nodded approval. "Very fair. Well, now that I've argued with you, fallen in the inlet, had coffee, made a sale for you and acted as Joe Fanelli's union advisor, my work here is done. Can I have a plastic bag for my wet clothes?"

He reached under the counter for one and handed it to her. "I'll close up for a few minutes and drive you home."

"No!" She put a hand to his chest. His heartbeat reacted to her touch. She must have felt it, because she dropped her hand immediately, then cleared her throat. "I'm perfectly capable of riding the Vespa home."

"Not a good idea after your dunking," he said, moving her aside when she stood in his path. "And I appreciate your lending a hand when I got busy. Thank you." He went to the door, changed the Will Be Back sign to read In Fifteen Minutes, then ushered her out ahead of him and locked the door.

"This is silly!" she argued, hurrying to keep up with him as he steered the Vespa toward his truck, then lifted it into the back.

"I…" she started to say, but he opened the passenger door and lifted *her* into the truck.

She growled and she pulled out the seat belt.

"As a general rule," he said, before closing her door, "socially correct women never growl. You might bear that in mind."

He had her home in five minutes, unloaded the Vespa and placed it for her in a corner of the garage. Behind her at a small distance, the beautiful yellow-and-white mansion that was her family's home was perched on a knoll, with a view of the vast lawn and the apple orchard. The house had a central cupola and porches at the front and back that exemplified the cozy style at the heart of everything Abbott. Janet seemed to fit in well.

The construction going on at the west end of the house reminded Brian again of the potential for scandal in his very name. His father had almost destroyed Chloe's addition. She'd wanted to enlarge the sun porch on the first level, add a room for Brian on the second level so that he could stay with them during holidays and other family occasions and expand the third floor so that when Sawyer and Sophie were married, there would be lots of room for her three children. Now Sawyer and Sophie were living at Sophie's place, nearer the hospital where she was a nurse, but Chloe had visions of having the entire family together in Shepherd's Knoll for holidays and long, lazy weekends, even though they all lived nearby.

His father had cruelly, vengefully set fire to the addition though it was obvious that both China and Chloe's wheelchair-bound Tante Bijou were inside. The building had gone up quickly, and had it not been for China's courage and quick thinking, and the fact that Campbell and Winfield, who handled the estate's security, had arrived home at the right moment, both women might be dead. He shuddered at the thought.

"Thank you," Janet said. "Can you come over tomorrow?"

He had to pull himself out of his grim thoughts. Had he really agreed to be in this wedding? "Ah…why?"

"Because Abbott's West is sending someone from the

men's department to measure all of you for tuxes." Abbott's West was the retail flagship store in Manhattan.

He groaned. Yes, he *had* agreed. He'd done it for Janet, as much as for the family.

She widened her eyes at him teasingly. "If it's socially incorrect for women to growl, are socially correct men allowed to groan?"

She made him smile, but it seemed wisest not to answer. He knew this was going to get worse before it got better. "What time tomorrow?"

"Ten. And you'd better go easy on Joe Fanelli. You're going to need him a lot between now and the wedding." She patted his shoulder. "Thanks for the cookie and the coffee."

He sighed and smiled. "I don't regret that. But I'm starting to wonder if fishing you out of the water was the wisest thing I could have done."

"I guess only time will tell. See you tomorrow."

She headed for the house. He climbed into the truck to spare himself the view of her neat little backside as she walked away.

But there it was, beautifully framed in his rearview mirror.

Chapter Three

Janet congratulated herself on having handled the best-man issue well. Except for the falling-into-the-water part.

"You made him change his mind?" China asked in pleased surprise as Janet walked through the kitchen, heading for the stairs. China, in grubby jeans and shirt, looked as though she'd just come from the orchard, where she'd been working with Campbell since she'd arrived.

Janet and China were both average height and slender, with dark hair and eyes. But China had long hair, while Janet favored a short style that required a minimum of care. Cheerful smiles and carefully tended good looks lent them a similarity in appearance that had made it easy for them to pass as natural sisters. But close friends of Bob and Peggy Grant of Paloma, California, their adoptive parents, knew the girls had come to their home separately.

China's eyes went over Janet's shorts, T-shirt and lank hair. "How did your hair get wet? And you bought a new outfit?"

Janet explained about her impromptu dip, then the discussion that followed over coffee and cookies. She left out her insistence that she needed Brian's help to negotiate the murky waters of social correctness.

China took her arm as they went up the stairs. "He thought we'd be upset if the papers brought up his past?" she asked, incredulous as Janet explained his reluctance to be in the wedding. "It isn't his fault. And Susannah's part of this family's past whether Brian's involved or not."

"I know. But he cares a lot about the family, and doesn't want you to suffer or be embarrassed on his account."

"Wait till I get a hold of him," China threatened.

"Easy," Janet cautioned. "He's doing what you asked. I wouldn't scold him if I were you."

"True. But make sure Campbell doesn't hear that reason."

"I won't tell if you don't."

China stopped her at the top of the stairs. "Jan, thanks for doing this. Are you all right? I can't believe you fell in the water!"

Janet had been hoping her sister would focus more on her heroic accomplishment of getting Brian to agree, rather than her klutzy backward step.

"I'm fine," she assured her. "And Brian's going to be here at ten tomorrow morning for the tux fittings."

China gave her a quick hug. "You are a genius!"

"How many times have I told you that?" Janet teased. "So, how are things in the orchard? Is the Duchess ready for harvest?"

The Duchess was the largest tree in the vintage section of the apple orchard. The trees in that area had been a gift from Thomas Jefferson to the early owners of the property. Campbell watched over the entire orchard with great care but devoted particular attention to the old trees.

China had spent almost a month working with him while waiting for Chloe to come home from Paris so that China could take the DNA test to prove she was Abigail Abbott. Killian and Sawyer had been convinced of her honesty, but Campbell had suspected that she was lying.

Killian's decision that China work on the estate with Campbell in the interim had been intended to help them get acquainted, but they'd disliked each other and warred continually.

Then the DNA test had proved that she wasn't an Abbott. China had come to Shepherd's Knoll in the first place because of a box she'd found in the attic of their adoptive father's home after he'd died. The sisters had been cleaning out the house to put it on the market and found two cardboard storage boxes hidden in the eaves. One had China's name on the lid and the other Janet's.

China's had contained clippings of the Abbott toddler's kidnap, a pair of rompers made by Abbott Mills and a homemade rag doll.

Janet's had held a birth certificate and several other things that had led her on a search to Canada while China had come to Losthampton.

When it became clear that China wasn't Abby, everyone wondered why her box had been filled with clippings about Abby's abduction. Then Campbell suggested that perhaps the lids of the boxes had been accidentally switched at some point, during one of the times the Grant family had moved, and that the contents might actually be clues to Janet's family.

China had sent for Janet and her DNA test had proved that Abigail Abbott was finally home. It also allowed the antagonism that had existed between Campbell and China to turn to attraction, since they weren't related after all and, eventually, to love. Janet was thrilled to have found her family but envied the look in her sister's eyes.

"The orchard's coming along nicely. It's a waiting game at this point. We won't harvest until sometime in October. We're even going to get to go on our honeymoon."

Janet was fascinated by her sister's adaptation to life at Shepherd's Knoll. For a woman who'd made a living running a shopping service for other people, who loved going from store to store, mall to mall, checking the Internet for new products and following sales, she'd settled with remarkable ease into this bucolic life.

"How lucky are we that we both belong here?" Janet asked her seriously as they walked down the corridor. "I'm not sure I could have stayed if you'd had to go." They'd made a deal, when each had set off on her search for her family, that whatever happened, they would remain sisters.

"You're Chloe's daughter, the little sister the guys have missed so much. I wouldn't have let you leave them again." They stopped at China's bedroom door. "But, had some writer created this story out of his imagination, it couldn't have worked out more perfectly for us. Now not only are we sisters, but we're going to be sisters-in-law. And double aunts to each other's children!"

China was apparently giddy over Janet's success with Brian. "I don't think there's any such thing," Janet laughed.

"Well, there should be."

"We are blessed. Are you finished work already?"

"No. But I saw you coming home and wanted to know what happened. I also wanted you to try on the dress for my wedding. You can wear the one we got for me when I was supposed to be a bridesmaid for Sawyer and Sophie."

"Ah, yes. In the simpler days before you and Campbell made it a double wedding." Janet started slowly backward toward her room at the end of the hall. "Okay. I'll shower quickly and wash my hair again. Brian didn't have any conditioner," she added as an aside. "Give me fifteen minutes."

Janet had Sawyer's old room on the northwest corner of the second floor. It had a view of the gardens and, in the distance, the hedges that separated Shepherd's Knoll from its neighbor.

The room was painted a subtle oyster color, and Chloe had redecorated it as a guest room, added a pink-and-white quilt and pink-flowered curtains. Janet had placed a few photographs around and, before leaving California, had shipped home some things she didn't want to put in storage. They would arrive in a couple of days.

She'd inherited an old maple hope chest that had been her adoptive mother's, and China had been willed a Boston rocker that had been their paternal grandmother's.

Janet thought wistfully of the Grants and wondered what they would have thought of the upscale lifestyle their daughters had become part of. They'd been happy, middle-class people. She was sure they'd had no idea who their adopted daughter really was. She wondered, as she often had since the DNA test had come back positive, how she'd gotten from here as a toddler to the doctor in Paloma who'd placed her with the Grants.

She shook off a stab of sadness and tried to accept that this was a mystery she might never be able to solve.

In the shower, Janet's thoughts turned to Brian. He was right that his position as bastard son of the scandalous Susannah would always be a tagline for the press. She felt a little guilty for manipulating him into a position where the subject was bound to come up again—in print.

But while he knew the Abbotts would always welcome him, she doubted that he understood how little they cared about that information resurfacing during the wedding.

So in reality, she told herself while working a rich conditioner through her short hair, she was performing a service for him. He had to see it happen, to be a part of their happiest times, to realize how much he was loved anyway.

Thus far, his life had been grim. China had told her that when Susannah Stewart had died in London shortly after Brian was born, the chauffeur she'd run off with had called Corbin Girard to tell him about his motherless son. But Girard had been out of the country and his wife, Frances, had taken the call.

Frances, a scrupulous woman, had sent for the baby, and when Corbin had arrived home insisted they raise the boy. Corbin had hated Brian for reminding him of the mistake he was unable to escape. And while Frances loved Brian, he reminded her every day of her husband's faithlessness. Brian claimed to have been confused as a child by the sadness in her eyes when she looked at him.

He was in desperate need of a large dose of good cheer. Preparations for a double wedding would certainly provide that.

She wrapped a towel around herself and left the bathroom, to find Chloe placing a large crystal bowl of white roses on a crocheted doily on top of the old mahogany highboy in the corner. She turned to smile at Janet, her heart in her eyes as it always was when she looked at her.

"I thought you might like these," Chloe said with a soft smile. She was petite, with short gray hair in a smooth style and a still-beautiful face with smile lines and artfully applied makeup. She wore the outfit Janet had brought her from the Joshua Burke outlet in L.A. Chloe usually wore gauzy, loose-fitting gowns around the house, and tailored suits when she went out. But Janet had fallen in love with the soft pink cropped pants and cropped jacket she'd known would flatter her mother's still-slender figure.

"Thank you. They're exquisite. And that looks wonderful on you." The color pinked her cheeks and brightened her dark eyes.

"When you were a baby," Chloe said, handing her a

light eyelet robe, "you loved to give things—your bottle, your doll, the shirt off your back quite literally. Your father used to tease that you were a bad advertisement for Abbott Mills products because you were always taking off your clothes." Her voice quieted and her eyes filled. "And this is my first gift from my grown daughter. Thank you, *ma chère*. I'm thrilled that you thought of me."

"It was my pleasure." Janet belted the robe and went to hug her mother. "You've been so good to me and China."

Chloe dismissed that with a very Gallic wave of her hand. "You're my daughter. And we thought China was, too, for a while, and have decided that she will remain one. I'm so happy she's marrying Campbell, because now I can still claim her as part of the family." She looped an arm in Janet's. "Kezia's made scones. Will you join us for tea? All the girls are up and waiting to hear how you convinced Brian to be in the wedding."

Kezia was the Abbott's African-American cook and housekeeper. She and her husband, Daniel, the chauffeur, had been with the Abbotts since before Killian was born. A handsome couple, they had the status of family. While Daniel tried to remember what he considered "his place," Kezia thought hers was in the thick of things and offered her opinion and counsel on all manner of issues, whether asked to or not.

"I'll be right there," Janet promised. "As soon as I've put some clothes on."

Chloe, one hand on the doorknob, studied Janet with suddenly pointed interest. "China tells me you fell into the water."

Janet reached into the closet to avoid Chloe's gaze. Though they'd been separated most of Janet's life, she had a mother's gift for reading her daughter's mind.

"I was distracted," she said, pulling a pale blue shirt out of the closet. She reached into a drawer for matching shorts.

"You find Brian distracting?"

"We were arguing. That's what distracted me."

"What did you say to make him change his mind?"

"I heaped guilt upon him."

Janet tossed the clothes on her bed, expecting Chloe to scold her for doing such a thing. Instead, her mother grinned.

"Well done. I'm never afraid to use guilt in a pinch, if I'm sure it'll bring about the right result." She blew Janet a kiss. "It is true that the apple never falls far from the tree. An apt metaphor around here in more ways than one. Hurry, *chérie*. Killian wants to talk to you, but don't let him keep you too long or all the scones will be gone. He's in the library."

Dressed and feeling triumphant that she'd been able to accomplish something for Killian by encouraging Brian to join the wedding party, she went downstairs to the beautiful, quiet room Killian used as an office when he was home. It opened onto the rose garden, where Chloe had picked the blooms she'd placed on the high-boy in Janet's room.

But Killian didn't seem surprised that Janet had convinced Brian.

"I heard," he said when she tried to tell him about it. He gestured her to a plump sofa. "China told me. Well done. I knew he'd listen to you. But, you're the one I want to talk about."

She wasn't sure whether to be pleased or nervous. Her situation here, though she felt fairly secure in it, was still so new that she half expected it to come crashing down on her at any moment. She waited for him to go on.

"I realize it's early yet and you deserve some time to get your bearings," he said, coming to sit beside her, "but when you're ready to go back to work, I'd like you to think about working for Abbott Mills. You'd find the family business challenging and a good place to spread your wings as a businesswoman. You have an impressive history with Watson, Dunn and Crawford."

She pretended to frown at him. He was known for the research he put into projects of any description. "You looked me up?"

"I look everything up," he admitted. "You've been in the business only four years, but you had some very happy clients and bosses who raved about your accomplishments. At a time when no one can predict what the market will do, you were making investors money."

"The market's fairly simple to analyze…" she began.

"No, it's not," he argued. "It's difficult and painstaking, but you seem to have a gift for it. I'd have probably been able to pick you out as an Abbott even before the DNA test proved you one."

She shrugged away the compliment. "We had a business class in high school and one of our projects was to pick a few stocks and follow their progress. I won some and lost some but tapped a real enthusiasm for the process. I kept the interest up in college and had so much fun with it I knew I'd make a career of it."

She heard the words come out of her mouth and wondered what had happened to the woman she'd been just a little over a month ago. She was still Janet Grant, but she felt as though discovering the Abbotts had changed the shape of her life. No, she wasn't really Janet anymore. She was Janby, a composite of then and now.

Killian's offer touched and flattered her, but business was the last thing on her mind right now.

"Will it disappoint you if I decide to do something else?" she asked candidly. "At least for a while."

He considered a moment. "Only in that it's so great to have you back and to discover that you're a lot like I am. I'd miss the time it'd give us together. It makes me wonder what our lives would have been like if we'd grown up together, instead of my feeling responsible for the fact that you were taken."

Every other thought in her head dissolved at that casual admission. She hitched a knee up on the sofa cushion to turn toward him and look him in the eye.

"What?" she asked.

He shook his head and prepared to stand, but she put a hand to his arm to hold him there. "Killian…"

"Doesn't matter." He placed a fraternal hand over

hers. "It's not important. It's just interesting to speculate on what might have been."

She saw a line form between his eyes, and detected a definite tension in his shoulders. "How could you possibly have been responsible for the fact that I was kidnapped?" she insisted.

"Janby…"

"Please tell me."

He expelled a breath and leaned back again. "I was a tense little kid," he said with another shrug, obviously trying to make light of what he was about to say. "And the oldest. I felt responsible for everything. Now, about your working for us…"

She folded her arms. "I want to talk about this. Don't think you can put me off."

He rolled his eyes. "God, you're Campbell all over. Part Abbott, part bull terrier. He never lets anything go, either."

"In some instances, that can be a good thing." She smiled. "Please. I'd like to understand."

"Okay, but it's pretty simple, and not all that dramatic except in how it affected me."

She nodded in acceptance of that and he went on.

"You know that Sawyer's and my mother left when we were very small. She was pregnant with Brian, thanks to Girard, but he wouldn't leave his wife for her, so she took off with the chauffeur. No one suspected she was pregnant at the time, or that Girard was involved."

"Yes, China told me."

"Well, I couldn't believe my mother wasn't coming

back." He stared across the room, the memories playing themselves out on some screen Janet couldn't see. "Every night for years, I sat at my window and watched for her to return. I was sure she'd miss me. Even after your mother married our father, I was sure Susannah would return one day."

"But she didn't."

"No. She died right after Brian was born, but we didn't know that. Anyway, the night you were taken, I joined a sleepover at a friend's house. Your mother was wonderful and I was finally beginning to realize that she loved me more than Susannah ever did. So I left my post and went to the party." He turned to her, speaking the words as if searching for absolution. "And you were kidnapped. Had I been looking out that window, I might have seen someone approach the house or leave with you."

She took his hand and squeezed it, feeling just a little of what he must have suffered. "Oh, Killian. I'm so sorry. What a burden you've placed on yourself, when it wasn't your fault at all."

He nodded glumly. "I know. But I was a kid whose mother left him without a second thought. I was sure I had to be pretty bad. It was easy to blame myself for yet another family tragedy."

Tears filled her eyes and burned her throat. She imagined a serious little boy burdened by all that darkness. And she realized for the first time all the love that must have been hers when she was born.

He saw her brimming eyes and gave her his handkerchief. "Please don't cry. It's all over now. And it wasn't just me. We all felt responsible. Sawyer thought he was the stand-in big brother since I was gone, so it was his fault. And Campbell threw you out of his room that afternoon because you were a destructive little devil and broke one of his precious trucks. So he had to live with the knowledge that his last contact with you was a shout for your mother to get you out of his room."

She absorbed this information with quiet dismay.

"But all's well that ends well," he said, suddenly brisk. "We shouldn't even be talking about this when we're so, so lucky to have you back."

"I'm the lucky one. Now I feel guilty that you all beat yourselves up because of me."

He leaned over to wrap her in a hug. "That would *really* be silly. We all have to focus on the fact that you're back, not that you were gone."

That made sense. Still, she hated the mystery that had caused her family so much pain. Though she'd been the victim, she'd escaped relatively unscathed. She found that upsetting. But Killian seemed to be trying to put the past behind them and she wanted to support him. "You're absolutely right," she said.

"I am. And try to give some thought to how much fun it would be to work together." He stood, offered her a hand up, then walked her toward the kitchen, telling her about the companies that made up the conglomerate of Abbott Mills, and the different ways her talents could be put to good use. She smiled and gave him her full attention, but she was troubled by what he'd told her.

JOE FANELLI WAS several inches shorter than Brian and more thickly built. He helped Brian restock the shelves after closing, a frown of concentration on his face. Considering he was putting laundry detergent on the same shelf with canned vegetables, Brian figured his focus wasn't working.

Brian opened two refrigerated colas and invited Joe to join him at the chairs near the potbellied stove that occupied the middle of the shop. Joe looked surprised. "I'm almost finished," he said, holding up his last bottle of detergent.

Brian nodded. "But look at where you're putting it."

Joe turned back to the shelf. His head tipped back in exasperation. "I'm sorry," he said, gathering up bottles. "It'll just take me a—"

"That can wait a few minutes," Brian insisted. "We haven't had much time to talk since I hired you." He held up the cola invitingly. "Come and sit down."

Joe took the place opposite Brian, a dark blue apron over his jeans and white T-shirt emblazoned with the store's logo. He looked wary as he accepted the can of soda.

"You're going to tell me I'm not doing a good job," he said, slightly defensive.

"No," Brian corrected him. "When we work together, you do a very good job. But over the next couple of weeks, I'm going to have to leave you alone for a few hours every few days. My friend's getting married and I'm going to be in the wedding. Lots of fussy stuff to do."

Joe smiled hesitantly. "The Abbotts?"

"Yes."

"My mom's been talking about it. She's helping my grandfather with the catering. She says you don't see a double wedding every day."

"Yeah. That's why I asked you to work tomorrow morning. I have to get fitted for a tux."

Joe made a face. "When you're used to shorts and T-shirts, a tux makes you feel like you're choking."

Brian remembered. "I used to have to wear one a lot. I even had my own. It does feel like you're going to strangle."

Joe nodded, his manner relaxing. "When you were in the November Corporation? Before your father—" He stopped abruptly, his face going pale. "I'm sorry."

"It's okay." Brian took a swig of cola. "I know people talk about it. Life's full of all kinds of things you can't do much about, and, unfortunately, people find gossip interesting. Probably because they all have their own problems, and they like to talk about stuff that doesn't affect them."

Joe seemed surprised by that candor, then a flush replaced his pallor. "Yeah, I know."

"My concern," Brian said, "is that the good work you do while I'm watching you doesn't change when I'm not around."

Joe's flush deepened. "That woman complained," he guessed, "about the afternoon you went to Springfield."

Before Brian could concur that it was Mrs. Lindell, Joe went on to describe her. "Short, round lady with big, old-fashioned hair?"

"Yes. Mrs. Lindell. I've only owned this place a couple of months, but she's been coming here for years, and we want her to keep it up."

"I'm sorry." Joe appeared sincere. "I knew she was going to be mad. She was trying to find this hair stuff I never heard of, and I took her to where we stock hair products. Then Natty called—that's my girlfriend—and she wanted to talk about this…this problem we're having." He lowered his eyes and picked at the rim of the can with his thumbnail. "I tried to tell her I was busy, but we have a big problem and I…I felt like I had to listen. For that minute…it was more important than the work."

At this point, Brian wished he didn't know what Joe's problem was. It would have been easier to tell him that when he was on the job, nothing was more important than the work. But he was Brian Girard, not Corbin. He knew there were times when life was much more important than work, no matter whose livelihood was at stake. Particularly when a woman and a baby were involved.

"Can I promise to do better?" Joe asked hopefully. "I like working here and I really need this job."

"And I really need someone to help me out. But I have to be able to depend on you."

"I know, I know," Joe said eagerly. "I promise you can. I'll tell her not to call me unless it's an emergency."

"Tell her you'll call her when it's slow. But if you get busy, you'll have to call her back."

"I will." He looked relieved and sat forward in his chair. "She's been kind of…well, she's sort of…" He suddenly gave up trying to talk around it and said with a deep breath, "She's pregnant. Our parents are totally freaking out, but I'm okay with it. I'm staying home from school so I can save some money so we can get married. But my parents want me to go to school. They say they'll pay for everything. I want to, though. She's my girl. It's my baby."

Brian had to commend him for his attitude, but wondered if Joe had a realistic idea of what he was up against. And what it would cost.

"Do you have insurance that'll help with this?"

"No. But I'll work hard. The trouble is, we were going to wait to get married until I could afford an apartment and a car, but her parents want her to give the baby up for adoption. She's really upset. Her parents are nice people, but they don't understand that we really love each other and we want this baby." He firmed his jaw. "So you can take all the time off you want, and I'll be happy to fill in for you 'cause I could use the extra hours, and I'll do everything the way you would do it. Don't worry."

Brian felt for his innocence, while still applauding a sense of responsibility that wasn't always in evidence among kids Joe's age.

"Tell you what," he said. "If you do a good job for me—take care of our customers and keep the shelves stocked and the place clean—maybe we'll have to talk about a raise."

The boy was stunned, then his face split in a wide grin. "That'd be cool," he said.

"Okay. After you finish stocking, then you can go home. I've got a few orders to place before I leave tonight."

Brian went into his small, cluttered office, all that talk about babies reminding him that he'd intended to lay in more baby supplies. He had diapers and wipes, but mothers were always asking for baby food, teething biscuits, pacifiers. He pulled out a catalog he'd saved from the score that came in every day and settled down to review it and make some choices.

The cover of the catalog featured a young woman with long dark hair and a young baby on her hip. The woman reminded him of Janet and he was instantly distracted.

He remembered how panicky he'd felt when she'd fallen into the water and he couldn't spot her. He imagined his response had been a simple human reaction to a life in danger.

But there was a little tremor at work even now in the pit of his stomach when he thought about her. He could recall precisely the gratitude in her eyes when she'd opened them and looked into his. Her eyelashes wet and clumped in spear points, and her hands had clung to his arms. Clearly, she'd been happy he was there.

Sentimentality had been killed in him at an early age by his father, who had no use for thoughts or feelings that didn't result in more money for the November Corporation or more power for himself. Still, Janet Grant Abbott made him feel…hell, he didn't know what it was. Was there a name for excitement mingled with reluctance?

He was trying to keep an emotional distance from the Abbotts that would be healthy for both of them. But, whether deliberately or not, she was drawing him in. He could make a fuss and pull away, an approach that was so lacking in style and dignity.

He had to just keep to himself during all this wedding stuff. He could be courteous without being vulnerable. The one thing that could make his future iffier than it already was, was a woman.

He'd had numerous relationships in the past, but except for a tender crush on Cordie in the days before she even knew Killian, none of them had ever been serious. They'd been for sex or fun or ego maintenance.

A relationship with Janet would be different. But she'd just found a dream life and so had he, really, but they were social strata apart. Feelings for Janet were best ignored.

He had a vague memory of having told himself that before.

He'd pay closer attention this time.

Chapter Four

Janet, China, Chloe and Kezia sat in a circle on the living-room floor, making hanging votive holder favors for the reception. Cordie, Killian's wife, who was a tall redhead seven-and-a-half-months pregnant with twins, a boy and a girl, was unable to get down to the floor. She sat on the sofa with her cat in what was left of her lap. Versace was an enormous long-haired gray who was having a great time swiping a paw at the jewelry wire Cordie worked with to create hangers for the votives. Tante Bijou's wheelchair was pulled up to a place in the circle. She was a plump little woman who'd practically raised Chloe. She'd been in the French Resistance as a girl, written a book about it and had been married several times.

Chloe had gone to visit her several months ago, discovered she was ill, stayed to help nurse her back to health, then brought her back to Shepherd's Knoll to continue her recovery.

Even wheelchair bound, Bijou, a lively old woman with a lot of jewelry and apricot-tinted hair, contributed to the family's get-togethers—in French.

"Will Sophie have to work right up to her wedding day?" Kezia asked. A box of votive candles rested on her ever-present white apron.

"No." China cut jewelry wire into long strips. "Tomorrow's her last day until they come home from their honeymoon. Then she's going to give serious thought to quitting the hospital and helping Sawyer with foundation work."

"She has so much to do with the children, and the remodeling."

Because Sophie and the children loved their old home, Sawyer was having it remodeled by a local architect, famous for his Craftsman designs. It had reached chaos stage, and they were all moving into Shepherd's Knoll, on the third floor, now being readied for their occupancy, until the house was completed.

"I'd give anything for a nanny-cam in Mom's room," Cordie said, cutting lengths of ribbon. "Imagine all those gorgeous men in their underwear, talking baseball and the stockmarket."

"We could talk about the stockmarket." Janet took a length of jewelry wire from Cordie, added a bead, then made a decorative twist in the wire and added several more. She knotted one end and passed the wire to Chloe. "I happen to know Abbott Mills stock is up a half because of strong sales reported last quarter."

Cordie handed her a length of ribbon. "I always think stockbrokers should look like Killian—three-piece suits and concerned expressions. Did you find the work exciting?"

Janet thought back on her successful career, remembering it as if it were a story about someone else. The past month had changed everything about her life—even a few things about her.

"It was," she replied. "And it was edgy because you're always dealing with someone else's money. I tried to keep that in mind all the time, so that when I was being creative or inventive with a purchase, I was never foolish. Still, you make mistakes sometimes, and underneath all my fancy work, somebody's life savings, or at least the part of it they're willing to take a chance on, is at stake."

"That sounds so scary to me." China attached the beaded wire to a wire loop under the neck of a glass votive holder.

"It's a lot like your business." Janet held the glass steady while her sister worked. "I went shopping with other people's money, just as you did."

"The only difference being," Kezia said gravely, putting candles in the votive holders they'd already completed, "that she might not get the best bargain if she wasn't careful, but she didn't really stand to lose *all* their money."

Janet nodded. "True. But that doesn't happen as often as you'd imagine. We respect the wishes of clients who are conservative, and take risks for those who are willing. But right now…" She handed Kezia the finished holder. "I'm happy not to have to think so hard."

Chloe smiled gently from across the circle. "You have other things on your mind, *chérie?*"

Janet didn't want to talk about what she'd been think-ing, reluctant to cast shadows on this fun, creative day.

"Nothing important to votive-holder making." She concentrated on threading wire into a blue glass bead.

China elbowed her, causing her to miss the hole. "We can talk about other things. Give."

Janet elbowed her in return. "I don't want to. We have a hundred more of these to make."

"And a whole week to finish them. What are you worried about?"

"I'm not worried," she corrected China, though everyone else seemed to be. They looked up from their work, waiting for her to speak, and Tante Bijou asked Chloe a question in French, to which Chloe shook her head and indicated Janet, clearly waiting for her to explain. "Okay. I'll just tell you briefly, then we don't have to talk about it again until after the wedding."

China frowned at her. "My wedding doesn't stop *your* life. What? Tell us what you're thinking."

Clearly, Janet would not escape without sharing what was on her mind. "Killian and I were talking yesterday. He said he thought it would be fun if I joined the company, because he found it interesting that we have a lot of traits in common, one of them being a fascination with business."

"Oh, Janby," Chloe said, after a swift interpretation of that information to Tante Bijou, "he would love it if you joined the company, but he wouldn't want you to do it just because—"

"No, no, that isn't it," Janet interrupted. "He wasn't

trying to coerce me. It was something else he said that got me thinking."

Everyone waited for her to go on.

"He said," she continued, "that he wondered what our lives would have been like had I not been taken, and had he not grown up feeling responsible for the fact that I was."

She waited for them to look as horrified about that as she was, but instead, they all seemed to accept it. She couldn't imagine why. Because they'd all dealt with it longer, she supposed, whereas she'd only known for about a month that she'd been the victim of kidnap.

"Not only that." She had to make them understand what she felt. "But Sawyer and Campbell have felt guilty, too, though for different reasons."

"Yes, *ma chère*." Chloe and all her companions leaning toward Janet in the circle. Cordie placed her hand on Janet's shoulder from behind her on the sofa. "But they've all adjusted. At the time, it was very hard for everyone, but none of that matters now."

"You still don't know who took me," Janet noted. "I thought if I could get to the bottom of it, my brothers would feel…absolved."

There was a communal objection. Kezia said firmly, "Janby, I was here then. The police spent days looking for clues, for anything that would lead them to who took you, and they found nothing. Don't do this to yourself."

"Please, Janet," Chloe said urgently. "You're home! We got over the frustration of having no way to find you, and God brought you back. The boys have found love, and they've always had purpose, so life will be good again at Shepherd's Knoll."

Janet heaved a sigh. They didn't understand that this was going to be her purpose. That was all right. Obviously, this was something she would have to do without assistance or even approval.

She smiled at her mother. "Okay, then. We'll forget it. I just didn't want the boys to feel guilty because of me."

"They're happy because of you, because you're home," Cordie said, squeezing her shoulder. "Don't worry about the past. Everybody's looking forward."

"Okay. Forward it is."

She let the subject drop, and the votive-holder project was resumed in earnest, finished ones placed on the table by Tante Bijou, who wheeled her way to the dining room and back. They talked about the latest names in contention for Cordie and Killian's twins, and China and Campbell's delight that Brian had changed his mind about serving as best man.

"Janet charmed him," China said.

Janet pretended boredom. "It's such a trial to be irresistible."

"Actually, they were arguing, she backed away from him and fell in the water," China revealed to gasps of concern and several shouts of laughter. "He felt so sorry for her that she's so clumsy that he agreed to come and keep an eye on her."

As everyone smiled over that, Janet thought it remarkable that China was so close to the truth. Still, she was going to make the best of her opportunity to spend time with him.

"THANKS FOR changing your mind about the wedding," Campbell said to Brian as they started down the stairs. The fittings were completed, and the tailor was on his way back to Abbott's West. Killian had taken over Campbell's office for a call to London and Sawyer had gone to Sophie's to check on the progress of the remodel. "I know there's a lot of time-consuming fuss involved, but Mom and all the ladies are working on it so hard that I don't want to seem unenthusiastic."

Brian understood completely. "Yeah. It's not a problem. I hired someone for the store, so I suddenly have more time than I expected to have."

"Well, I appreciate your spending it on this kind of stuff. Do you have a couple more minutes?"

"Yes. You probably want to take me to lunch for my outstanding service."

"We could do that," Campbell agreed. "We haven't had fried clams in a long time. But I wanted to show you where China and I are going to put our house."

"Great."

Laughter and conversation came from the women gathered in the middle of the floor, Cordie on the sofa and Tante Bijou in her chair, all forming what appeared to be a production circle.

"All finished measuring?" Chloe asked as Campbell and Brian wandered over to look down at their project.

"All finished," Campbell confirmed. "You won't believe how fat Killian's gotten."

Chloe shook her head over his teasing. "He hasn't gained an ounce. You're just always trying to make trouble."

Cordie patted her belly. "If he has, it's sympathetic pregnancy. He'll be svelte again after I deliver. Where is he?"

"In my office, talking to London." Campbell walked around the circle to where China sat and squatted behind her. "You ladies still going to Fulio's for lunch?"

"Yes," China replied, turning to kiss him. "Sophie's going to meet us there. Lunch is a gift from Fulio."

"Okay. Then I'm taking Brian to lunch after I show him the site for the house."

"Have fun, but don't eat too much. Fulio's sending a few different kinds of cake home with us so we can decide which one we want."

"Will there be one cake or two at the wedding?"

"One big one."

"Two would simplify the decision-making process."

"One cake. Be ready to sample."

While China and Campbell kissed again, Brian looked away and caught sight of Janet studying him. The expression in her eyes was curiously analytical, and he couldn't quite decide what to make of it. He simply smiled.

She waved a length of wire with beads on it. "Where are you guys going for lunch?"

"Yvonne's," Brian replied. "I have a thing for fried clams. Add an order of fried asparagus and it's to die for."

China made a face. "You take something healthy like asparagus and deep-fry it? That's criminal."

He frowned at Campbell. "You've never treated her to fried asparagus?"

"I'll have to bring some back to her."

"That's not the same as having it fresh."

"We could all go sometime," China said.

Cordie rolled her eyes and tapped her stomach. "I'd have indigestion for days. And Sophie's eating nothing but salad till after the wedding. The four of you should go."

The four of you. Clearly, Cordie was adding Brian and Janet to Campbell and China. They'd been paired up—at least until after the wedding.

"I'd love to try it." Janet cast a friendly glance in Brian's direction. There was nothing remotely seductive or predatory about the suggestion, but something in the smile made him feel like a man on borrowed time. "Why don't we go tonight?"

"Can't tonight," Campbell said. "We have a meeting with the builder at seven-thirty. It was the only time he could fit us in. Then we're pretty much booked with one thing or another until the wedding." Campbell got to his feet, blew China another kiss and led the way through the kitchen.

He walked Brian along the path through the orchard, now fragrant with the smells of fruit, salt from the ocean mixed with late-summer air and cooking fires to create the beach's unique perfume.

Campbell stopped about twenty yards from a hedge that separated the Abbott property from the Girards. "A back lawn right here," Campbell said, "with picnic table, swings."

"Canopied glider swings, or kids' swings?"

"Both." He pointed off to the side. "Playground equipment over there, lawn swings over here." He walked forward, obviously pacing off an area. "Six steps up to a deck that stretches across the back. Gas grill, picnic table, deck chairs."

Campbell spread his arms, and Brian could tell he'd left him and was living in his house plan. "Forty-eight hundred square feet," he said. "Four bedrooms—three upstairs, one down—three-and-a-half baths. Ten-foot ceilings. All the usual stuff, plus a garden bath off the master bedroom downstairs, a morning room off the kitchen just because Sophie's always wanted one, a gallery for use as a library that is open to the living room, which has a vaulted ceiling. A columned porch in the front, eventually with wisteria."

Campbell sighed, finally coming back to the open field. He pointed ahead to the orchard. "And a great view of the apples. What do you think?"

"I can see myself with a gin and tonic," Brian replied, "in a chair under the wisteria."

Campbell nodded thoughtfully. "I feel like I belong in it, and it isn't even up yet."

"That's because you know China will share it with you and fill it with kids."

Campbell grinned at him. "Two will be good."

"From what I've observed of other people's children, two can pretty much fill up a place."

Campbell paced off an area, beckoning Brian to follow him. He finally stopped and sat down in the grass. "This is the front porch. No gin and tonic, I'm afraid, but have a seat and tell me what you think of the view."

Brian sat, leaving a few feet between them. The breeze was warm and filled with the scent of the orchard. "I think you've picked the perfect spot," he said, breathing deeply and letting the bountiful smells fill his being.

"You have a pretty spectacular place." Campbell drew up his knees and folded his arms on them. "When we were kids, we used to pass your grandmother's house and imagine that people from another time lived there. It appears to belong in the nineteenth century, complete with the old roses draped along the fence."

Brian's mother's mother had left him a wonderful Gothic Revival home. It was enormous, with architectural details befitting nobility. He'd been rattling around in it all by himself for the past six months or so, wondering whether to keep all the fussy old furnishings or bring in something lighter that might look out of place.

Selina Carter had been tall and thin and not very pretty, but always warm and loving to Brian. She and his mother, Frances, had been at odds over his father, but Brian and Frances had visited every Saturday and brought her groceries. She'd always had cookies for him and a warm hug he could feel today if he concentrated on it.

He'd so welcomed her embraces as a child. His mother had loved him and always been kind, but every once in a while he'd surprise an expression of sadness in her eyes. He hadn't understood then why she should feel sad when looking at him. He wasn't a perfect kid, but he'd worked hard in school and done his best to be cooperative. Though his efforts to do well had drawn criticism from his father, his mother always praised and encouraged him.

He just hadn't understood why he made her sad. Until his father wanted him to compete for The Man of the Year Award and Killian had beat out all the competition for it. His father had told him he was a failure despite his Girard genes, and he couldn't blame Susannah Abbott, because she'd been Killian's mother, too.

When Brian had turned to his father in confusion, the insult ignored in the face of a bigger issue, Corbin had been happy to tell him that his natural mother was Susannah Abbott.

"Can I have a cutting from the old roses?" Campbell asked. "I'll put a trellis in the back."

"Of course." Brian returned to the moment, thinking how lonely he might be right now if he hadn't been testing the seaworthiness of one of his rental canoes the day Sawyer was practicing one of his stunts to raise money for charity and had an accident.

Because Brian had helped save Sawyer's life, the Abbotts had adopted him in spirit at the same time that his father had disowned him. He wanted to feel like a part of their family but felt like a threat to their happiness, instead.

"You'll visit," Campbell said. It wasn't a question.

"Of course."

"You're not going to back off because I'm getting married."

"Back off?"

"The way you tried to do by not being in the wedding."

"I explained that."

"You did, but I don't believe you. While I love my brothers more than I could explain to anyone, and you and I share *no* blood, I relate to you because we have some of the same issues."

"I've never been arrested."

"Funny. That was a long time ago. You know what I mean."

"I do," Brian said, relenting. "I know exactly what it's like to feel out of place. The only difference between us now is that you've gotten over it."

Campbell said firmly, "If you feel out of place with us, you're doing it to yourself. Don't you remember telling me that night we drank champagne on the hood of the limo that you have to give up control and just let things be? That's what you have to do now. You're part of our lives. Stop trying to keep your distance. We're not afraid of you. Janet, particularly. She likes you."

Brian wasn't sure what to say to that. Campbell mistook his silence for confusion.

"You know, we're not afraid because your father's in a psychiatric hospital and may be going to jail, or because you're Susannah's out-of-wedlock son, or whatever. Just relax. You're in, whether you want to be or not."

Brian had to admire Campbell's insistence on having things his way. He was an Abbott. It just wasn't that simple. "Janet's very beautiful and capable, but my life's too new and complicated to invite someone else into it."

"Love isn't as complicated as you think."

"I remember when it was making *you* nuts."

Campbell laughed. "When you finally give in to it, you wonder why you fought so hard. Before that, I guess it is scary."

"Are you buying my lunch or not?" Brian asked, finished with the subject.

"Okay, okay. But do you want to go somewhere else if we're going to have to go back with the girls sometime?"

"No. You promised me the fried clams. I'd like them before it's time for dinner."

Chapter Five

In the week before the wedding, Janet went to the city with Chloe, Cordie and the brides to shop for honeymoon clothes. China and Campbell would be taking a Mediterranean cruise, and Sawyer and Sophie were going to Mexico. For someone who'd worked primarily with men, Janet found the sorority atmosphere of the shopping expedition was more fun than she'd had in ages.

At Abbott's West, summer clothes had been completely replaced on the racks with the rusty shades and thicker textures of fall and winter clothing. But Cordie, who'd once been a buyer for the store, took them into a back room where summer wear was stored, leaving Chloe and Janet to explore the new styles.

After lunch, Cordie led the way to the cosmetics department. She'd called ahead to warn them the Abbott brides and their parties were coming and reinforcements had been brought in to make sure each woman had special attention.

Janet had always been attentive to good grooming but owned only one foundation color, two shades of lipstick and a black mascara. The young woman helping her seemed to question the warm burgundy of her lipstick.

"What if you wear a cool color?" she asked. The woman was in her early thirties and flawlessly beautiful, her blue eyes shaded in a subtle lavender, her perfectly shaped lips glistening in a deep shade of red. Her black hair was caught back in a severe bun to show off her perfectly made-up features, and her glamorous look was dramatized by her white lab coat. The tag on the lapel read "Justine."

"I try to look cool?" Janet replied.

Judging by the woman's expression, that was not the correct answer. Justine set about educating her.

When they left in the middle of the afternoon, each woman had her own makeup case filled with colors appropriate to her complexion and preferred color palate—gifts from Killian and Cordie.

"And remember," Justine cautioned Janet, as though certain she needed to hear the words a second time, "the colors are coded on the label—*w* for warm, *c* for cool. Use the right ones for the optimum effect."

Janet couldn't help but wonder what the optimum effect was—and on *whom* it was supposed to be directed. Men, presumably. If she didn't mix her warms and cools, the male gender would be helpless to deny her anything.

She had no idea how Daniel found his way through the traffic with all the giggling and chattering going on in the back of the limousine. The women delved into their makeup kits, checked out each other's, admired Cordie's with its special colors suited to a redhead.

Then they passed around their clothing purchases

and, when they crossed the bridge to Long Island, settled back to talk about the brides' itineraries.

Sophie's parents lived in Vermont and weren't coming to the wedding because her father had recently broken an ankle, making travel difficult. Her mother had offered to watch the children while Sophie and Sawyer honeymooned, but with school starting, she thought it best to leave them with Chloe.

"You're sure you can do this, Chloe?" Sophie called to the front seat. She was small, her auburn hair caught back in a ponytail. "My father was a cop and he sometimes has trouble with them."

"I will do just fine," Chloe insisted over her shoulder, "and if I have any trouble, don't forget that Winfield is trained in self-defense."

Sophie nodded wryly. "That may come in handy."

From what Janet had observed, the children were smart and well mannered, but very lively.

The men were all gathered around the addition when Daniel pulled the limo up to the front of the house. The contractor promised that it would be painted in time for the wedding reception, though the inside would still be unfinished.

Winfield came to open one of the limousine doors while Daniel opened the other. Janet had found his powerful boxer's build, bald head and sometimes severe expression intimidating at first, but then she'd seen his gentle, protective manner with the family and the scrupulous way he worried about them, and decided that despite his appearance he was a pussycat.

The women joined the men to admire the work. It was a balm to the spirit, Janet thought, ridding them of the charred reminders of Corbin Girard's attempt to destroy Shepherd's Knoll.

"Well, isn't that going to look wonderful?" Chloe said, hands pressed to her heart as she walked up for a closer look. The walls had gone up and the building had begun to take the elegant shape it would have when finished. The sunporch remained open and was huge and somehow already inviting.

The three couples paired off. Janet would have gone inside, but she saw Brian, standing apart, and realized this was probably one unhappy reminder of his father. She went to stand beside him, hoping to distract him.

"Did you guys get together to play poker while we were gone?" she teased.

"No." He smiled, though his heart didn't seem to be in it. "Killian invited me over to add my name to his and Sawyer's and Campbell's on one of the beams before the addition was closed in."

"How nice. Some little successor a hundred years from now will be hiding his treasures in the wall and find your names."

He smiled over that. "Maybe one of Killian's twins' grandchildren."

"Wow. It's hard to imagine that far ahead."

"It's a nice thought, though. Especially when you're too used to looking back. What were you ladies up to all day?"

"Clothes and makeup," she replied. "Real girl stuff.

According to the woman behind the counter at Abbott's West, I've been wearing the wrong shade of lipstick all this time."

His eyes went to her lips and lingered there. It caused her heartbeat to slow to a tap. Then his eyes raised to hers, and she felt her heart might stop altogether.

"Do you want to try Yvonne's tonight?" he asked without warning.

"Ah…yes. But aren't we supposed to go with…?" She pointed toward Campbell and China.

"They have something going tonight…a meeting with the builder. I doubt we'll have another chance with them before the wedding."

"Okay."

"Six-thirty?"

"Sure."

Janet watched him say goodbye to everyone, then lope off toward his truck. It was a moment before she could close her mouth.

YVONNE'S WAS A SMALL, squarely built drive-in at the east end of Losthampton. It had no pretensions to fine dining, but simply provided a paper bowl of what Brian considered the world's best fried littleneck clams. There were a variety of side dishes available, but his preference was the fried asparagus.

Diners could eat inside on picnic tables in a relatively bare room, but he always took his food to go and went to the far end of Margaret Road and watched the water. He was usually alone there, even at the peak of tourist season because there was no beach at the end, just a shallow bluff covered with beach grass.

He'd brought a blanket from home, and had stored ice tea and soft drinks in the cooler in the back of his truck.

With Janet helping him spread the blanket, her shapely legs in simple jeans, a long-sleeved cotton sweater clinging to her small breasts, her hair loose and fragrant, he wished he hadn't decided to do this. His intention had been to stop her sending him those looks when she thought he was distracted, to make sure she understood that nothing could happen between them—if that was what she was thinking. Even though he hadn't stopped thinking about her since she'd come to the shop. She'd just been restored to the Abbotts and he ran a boat shack. Not to mention the fact that his natural mother had abandoned Janet's brothers, and his father had tried to burn their house down.

He'd help with the wedding as he'd promised, but his presence in her life seemed destined to have a negative effect.

She put a large natural-straw purse on one corner of the blanket, the bag from Yvonne's on another, and knelt down on the third while he went to retrieve the cooler.

It probably would have been better to let well enough alone and to simply fend off her interest—if he could even call it that—rather than make a point of it.

But when his father's attorney, a longtime family acquaintance, had called Brian to tell him his father's test results had caused sufficient concern that he'd be staying for a while at the psychiatric hospital in Boston, Brian had been surprised by his own distress.

Being invited to Shepherd's Knoll today to sign the beam and witness the repair of the damage his father had done had had a curative effect on one level, but on another, it reminded him of things that could never be.

What could he expect to share with Janet? Simple friendship?

That probably couldn't happen, either. And yet, here they were.

He placed the cooler on the empty corner, and she moved the paper bag to the middle of the blanket.

"This food has a lot to live up to," she said, opening the bag. "Seems Daniel and Kezia are Yvonne's junkies, too."

"You'll see for yourself. Iced tea? Cola?"

"Tea, please."

"Sweetened or un?"

"Un." She placed a paper bowl of clams and one of the bags of asparagus in front of him and accepted the bottle of tea.

Then, without preamble, she picked up a clam and bit it in half.

She rolled her eyes in approval.

"Dip it in the tartar sauce," he advised. "Then it's really heaven. The sauce is good with the asparagus, too."

She dutifully tried both. "Oh, good," she said dryly, "a new unhealthy habit. These are wonderful."

"I wouldn't steer you wrong."

"You backed me off the pier into the water," she challenged with a grin as she took another bite of clam.

"You can't blame me for that," he countered. "You did it all by yourself."

She curled up cross-legged and drew her food closer. "It was worth a shot. How's Joe Fanelli working out?"

"I think he's going to be okay. He told me about the baby. Thanks for the heads-up about that."

She appeared surprised by his gratitude. "You're welcome. I was afraid you thought I was butting in."

He grinned. "You were. You seem to like to do that. But in that case, it was a good thing."

"*And* in the case of the wedding."

"Yes, that, too."

"I'd say that, to this point my interfering has all been good."

Admitting that was probably dangerous, but he did. "So it seems."

"Is that why you invited me?" She was daring him. "To thank me?"

"I invited you," he replied, "to get you alone and ask you what's on your mind."

She blinked. "On my mind?"

"Yes." He had to get tough here. Make it clear. "You're up to something. I've watched you in action. You don't need anyone to prevent you from doing anything to embarrass the family. You're the epitome of class and style."

She didn't know whether to be pleased or angry. She started to speak a couple of times, then drew back and collected her thoughts. She put her food down and firmed her chin.

He prepared himself for her reaction.

"Okay, you want to be straight with each other?"

Not necessarily. He just wanted her to understand—

"I'm attracted to you," she said, interrupting his conversation with himself. "You're kind, smart, funny and comfortingly sane…when you're not being weird about embarrassing the family."

"But you're a poor judge of character, remember?" he said brutally. "You were left at the altar—"

"Would you do that to me?" she interrupted ingenuously.

"No, I wouldn't, because you'd never get me anywhere near an altar."

She took another clam and studied it, then looked up at him. "Are you a betting man?" she asked.

He closed his eyes, hoping to summon patience. "Janet, did you hear anything I told you about why I'm trying to keep my distance from your family?"

"I heard all of it." She popped the clam into her mouth and chewed. "Hogwash," she said finally.

"A 'kind, smart, funny and comfortingly sane man,'" he said, tossing her words back at her, "does not speak hogwash. Just because you don't like the truth doesn't make it any less true."

"You're telling me the same applies to me? That you won't admit to being attracted to me because you're afraid your birth history will somehow damage my future?"

"Yes," he said.

"Did I mention that that's a lot of hogwash?"

"Janet." He struggled to be patient. "I brought you here so we could talk about this like grown-ups."

"Really." She was rather amazing in a temper. He remembered it from the time she ran him over with the Vespa. But that time, he thought she'd been as angry with herself as she'd been at him. This time, he bore the full brunt of it. "Well, just how grown-up do you consider me, if you think I'd let such a thing affect my feelings for you?"

"Accepting someone else's refusal of a relationship is very adult."

"Hog—wash!" she said firmly, enunciating the syllables. "You're not saying you don't want to be involved with me. You're saying I shouldn't want to be involved with *you*. I think the adult thing would be to let *me* make that decision."

"Have you considered that it's possible I'm not attracted to you? Or doesn't the Abbott ego allow that?"

She was momentarily taken aback. "You're saying you're not?"

He could not have pulled off the lie. "I'm saying I don't want to be."

She looked relieved—and a little self-satisfied. "Well, that's not the same thing, is it?"

"It *amounts* to the same thing," he said. "We're two people in a wedding, and that's as far as it's going to go."

SHE LET THE ISSUE DROP. They could argue about what might or might not happen all evening, but the only thing that mattered was the moment of truth—and there would be one. He would turn to her, or she would turn to him, and the attraction he struggled so valiantly against would overtake his nobility.

And then she'd have him.

She was realizing more and more every moment how much she wanted him.

They finished their clams and asparagus while discussing the store, the wedding, the twins due in October. Their argument had released the tension and they talked with relative ease, she still cross-legged in the middle of the blanket, he stretched out and resting on an elbow, eating the frozen candy bars he'd brought for dessert.

They watched the sun set, then packed up their picnic, loaded it into the truck and headed for Shepherd's Knoll.

The matter of their attraction might have continued to lie dormant if he hadn't had to have the last word on it.

"I appreciate your seeing things my way," he said, then got out of the truck to walk around the hood and open her door.

"You changed your mind about being involved with the Abbotts because of *me*," she reminded him, accepting his hand as she leaped down. "I wouldn't light my victory fires yet."

She landed a little off balance in the tight space and fell against him.

She felt a thrum of reaction run the length of his body. His jaw tightened, as though he made a conscious effort to appear unaffected.

"You think a buttoned-up little stockbroker can seduce me?" he asked with an arrogance that wasn't like him at all.

She stared back at him a moment, let him believe that

remark had offended, and therefore discouraged, her. Then she caught his collar in a fist, stood on tiptoe and kissed him.

She teased him with the tip of her tongue, prodded his lips apart, explored inside, then got to the serious business of kissing him senseless.

He let that go on for half a minute, then he ripped her away from him. Sure that he intended to set her aside, get back into the truck and drive off, she dragged in a breath to steady herself.

Instead, he assumed control and kissed her in return, using all the tactics she'd applied, and a few that were uniquely his. One hand caught her hair, the other shaped her bottom, while his lips roamed her face, her throat and the neckline of her shirt.

When he finally let her go, they were both gasping for air.

"I changed my mind only about being in the wedding," he said, his voice a little shallow. "That's all."

"You're sure…that's all?" she whispered.

He drew a breath and closed the passenger-side door. "Maybe I have changed my mind about something else."

She was ready to be generous in victory. "What's that?"

"Maybe you're not so buttoned-down after all. Good night."

He turned in a wide circle and drove away.

She didn't know whether to laugh or cry.

Chapter Six

The wedding rehearsal was pandemonium until Father O'Neil took control of the loud group. The wisecracking Abbotts were forced into order as the priest dispatched the men like a field marshal to the front of the church and sent the women to the back.

He pointed to the organist at a small instrument to the side of the communion rail. She started the "Wedding March."

He then shouted over the formidable music. "You will leave half a length of the aisle between you as you walk up—one maid of honor, one bride, the second maid of honor, the second bride. Take your places."

Brian watched the women scramble into order at the back of the church—Cordie, then China, then Janet and Sophie. Chloe, Sophie's mother, Kezia and Daniel and Sophie's children turned to watch from the front pew.

"Oh, Lord!" Sawyer grumbled. "I'm going to marry China."

Campbell stepped out of line to make a switching motion with his hands at the same moment the women seemed to realize they were in the wrong order and took up the correct positions.

Campbell grinned at Sawyer. "No offense. I mean, I love Sophie, too, but I'm not eager to start out with three children."

"Killian has twins coming," Sawyer said under cover of the music. "You're going to be way behind."

"I'll catch up later," he promised. "Meanwhile, Brian isn't even in the running."

Killian leaned forward to confide, "Actually, he might be. I saw interesting things from my bedroom window last night."

Sawyer and Campbell turned toward him with sudden interest.

Brian threatened Killian with a look. "But, being the gentleman that you are, you're not going to talk about it, are you?"

"Not now," Killian replied, then at a stern glance from the priest for his whispering, he assumed an attentive stance. He added, as the priest shouted instructions at Cordie, first in line, "I'll tell them later that I saw you kissing Janet."

"You saw Janet kissing me," Brian corrected him.

"Janet didn't grab your back—"

"We are in a church!" Brian whispered, the admonition not as harsh as it should have been because he was distracted by the memory of that delicious moment. "Would you behave yourselves?"

"Hey," Sawyer said, weighing in. "She's our little sister."

"Yeah." Campbell, standing right beside him, elbowed him. "We'd like to know your intentions."

"At the moment," Brian replied, "my intentions are simply to survive this rehearsal!"

Father O'Neil cast an eye in Sawyer's direction as Sophie and her children reached the head of the altar. Sawyer moved quickly to take the children's place. The party paid closer attention.

Janet arrived next, in a loose-fitting flowered cotton dress. It appeared shapeless until she moved, then the fabric formed itself to her breasts and legs as she topped the steps and stood next to Cordie on the other side of the altar.

China arrived with her biological father, who was still so new to the role that he was almost as radiant as she was. He was average in height, with dark hair streaked with gray over his left eye. Hazel eyes looked over China as if he couldn't believe he'd found her. He'd driven from his home in Massachusetts to give her away.

"We say some prayers," the priest said. "Maids of honor raise the brides' veils and fold them back and take their bouquets, then use those kneelers. Groomsmen, kneel, too." He pointed to the kneelers on either side of the altar.

They did as he asked, then he gestured for them to get up. "Early in the Mass we perform the two wedding ceremonies—" he gestured them to come closer "—each couple moving to the bride and groom you're witnessing."

"Do you take this woman, yada yada, then we come to the part about the rings. You'll both have them," he told the best men firmly. "Two years ago we held up a ceremony for thirty-five minutes while the best man went home for the ring. Fortunately, the organist was a Beatles fan. But Mrs. Mitchell isn't."

The gray-haired organist shrugged cheerfully at the group.

"We'll finish Mass, we'll say some more prayers to bless you on your way, maids of honor give the brides their bouquets back, I turn you toward the parish community and introduce you to them as Mr. and Mrs. Abbott and Mr. and Mrs. Abbott…"

Chloe applauded dutifully and the children joined her.

"Then you're on your way, both bridal couples in front, first pair of witnesses next, then second pair."

Brian and Janet fell into line behind the other three couples.

"Are you a little tense?" Janet asked with a smile as she looped her arm in his. "You're not getting married, you know. Unless it's just that you're afraid because I kissed you last night."

"I kissed you," he corrected her. He heard his own words and remembered that he'd recently claimed to Killian that the opposite had happened, just as Janet had said.

"Okay! Stop at the door." Father O'Neil's voice brought them to a halt in the vestibule. "I assume the organist has your choices of music, that the flowers will be on time and that your photographer, whoever he is, will not flash light in my face or stand too close to me with his video camera?"

Killian assured him he wouldn't.

"And you'll have someone to control the press?"

"Our security man will be here."

"Excellent. Then do you have any questions of me?"

Everyone looked at everyone else and finally shook their heads in unison.

"Good. We'll all meet back here at ten a.m. sharp. Sleep well and don't worry about a thing. I've done a million of these. Everything will go beautifully."

A group of photographers already stood at the bottom of the steps and several mobile broadcast units were pulled up to the curb as the family left the rehearsal.

Brian knew that Killian's policy was tolerance of the press, unless their interest became harassment, in which case all bets were off.

While a television reporter spoke to the bridal couples, several photographers zeroed in on Janet, who was trying to make her way around the group to the limo.

She smiled, answered a few questions, then moved away, but one of them cut her off—a young man with a military haircut. Brian saw Killian and Sawyer look in her direction to see what the commotion was, prepared to go to her aid. Brian raised a hand to signal them to stay there, and went to intercept Janet.

As he reached her she was telling the reporter, her eyes flashing, that he was rude, even evil, to ask such a question.

Brian wrapped an arm around her, pushed the reporter aside and led her to his truck.

"What's your relationship to Miss Abbott, Mr. Girard?" someone shouted at their backs.

"Is there going to be *another* Abbott wedding in the future?" a second voice questioned.

Brian put Janet in the truck, then walked around to jump in behind the wheel. The kid stood in front of the truck to photograph them through the windshield.

Brian turned the key in the ignition and revved the motor. The reporter leaped for the sidewalk.

"Thank you," Janet said with a hand to her heart. "They're never satisfied with a few questions, but that Merriman asks the worst ones. I wish I could handle it like Killian does. The media never upsets him."

"That's because he outweighs you by about seventy pounds. They better not upset him. What did the guy ask you that made you try to leave?"

"He wanted to know if they'd written me into the inheritance yet," she said, resting her head back and closing her eyes, "and what my cut was. Do you believe it? He's the same one who chased me when I rode the Vespa to see you."

"I should have run him over," Brian said.

He headed for Fulio's, where the rehearsal dinner was taking place. The family was right behind them and they were all welcomed at the door by Fulio himself. He led them to the back and the new deck he'd built for summer evening parties.

Four tables had been placed end to end and set elegantly for dinner. Flowers and candles stood at intervals, and two chairs at both ends of the table were decorated with white ribbons for the brides and grooms.

A space had been set aside for dancing, and a small band welcomed the group with "Here Comes the Bride."

A festive mood took over the minor upset with the photographers as several of Campbell's and Sawyer's friends, who happened to be in the dining room, came to greet and congratulate them. Fulio began to bring hors d'oeuvres to the table and the band played nostalgic tunes from the sixties. Brian turned from making room for Tante Bijou's wheelchair next to Chloe's place at the table and saw Janet in the arms of one of Campbell's friends.

He knew Campbell, China and Janet all went out together and often met his friends. Janet and the young man didn't look intimate exactly, but they seemed very comfortable with each other—a situation he had to admit he envied.

He never seemed to strike the right note with her. Probably because there were places he didn't want their relationship to go—although he was sure the other day's kiss made it hard for her to believe that.

Chloe tugged on his sleeve until he sat in the chair beside her. "Is something going on," she asked with a maternal smile, "between my daughter and my pseudoson?"

He was surprised by the question, but even more surprised by the title she'd given him. "Pseudoson?" he laughed.

"I feel great maternal affection for you," she said, putting a hand on his arm, "even though I have no real right to. I want you to feel a part of this family, even though I understand you have reservations about belonging."

He must be the Abbotts' favorite topic of conversation. "Did Janet tell you that?"

"No, Campbell did. He thinks you're afraid you'll embarrass us because your presence naturally brings up Susannah."

"I don't understand where this comes from," he said with what he thought was credible confusion. "I attend every family event I'm invited to."

"Yes," she replied, "but you never just drop in as family would. You never come to us if you need something."

"I'm...very independent. You know my story, Chloe. I had a family, but my father disliked me and I made my mother sad. I learned to live on my own. I loved the November Corporation and wanted to be involved in that, but in the end that was denied me, too. So I'm just doing my own thing." He placed his hand over hers. "I do appreciate being included in your family. I'm just a man who goes his own way."

"Is that why you don't pursue Janet?" she asked gravely. "Or is it the embarrassment silliness?"

God. He needed a drink. "Neither," he replied. "She has to have time to get her bearings, and I'm sure when she has time to think about a relationship, she'll become interested in someone like the young man she's dancing with."

Chloe glanced up at them as another young man cut in. "The boy who's relinquished her," she said, "is Will Grantham. Campbell went to school with him. His father's from a wealthy family but he chose to join the ministry. He has a large congregation on Back Bay in Boston."

Imagining Janet with a minister's son was a little hard, but the rest of the package sounded right.

"I believe he's gotten two girls pregnant in the last year," she added. "I'd mail him in a crate to Dubai before I'd let her get serious about him."

"Wow. Is Dubai far enough?"

"Then there's the young man she's dancing with now."

"Yes?"

"Stone Scott. He's just finished his residency in pediatric medicine."

"That sounds very responsible."

"He's really very dull. In a life filled with children, all he talks about is his stock portfolio."

"Chloe…"

"Brian, Janet was lost to me most of her life. I will not see her involved with a man who isn't absolutely wonderful. You're my choice."

"Thank you. But shouldn't the choice be hers?"

Chloe smiled as though she knew something he didn't.

STONE SCOTT HAD BEEN aptly named, Janet thought. His stocks-and-bonds conversation had all the warmth of a discussion with a block of granite. She might have found it interesting from a former stockbroker's perspective, except that his insistence on crediting his own superior skills was making her comatose. Desperate to escape, she gestured madly in Brian's direction when they passed his chair.

She saw her mother lean toward Brian and whisper something that made him smile. But he wasn't moving.

Please, she mouthed to Brian over Stone's shoulder as he whirled her around.

The next moment he tapped Stone on the shoulder.

Stone looked disappointed. She smiled graciously and turned into Brian's arms before Stone could object.

"Thank you!" she said, wrapping both arms loosely around his neck. "My IQ's gone down ten points listening to all his successful stock ventures."

She half expected Brian to hold her stiffly, since he was so determined to resist her, but he held her confidently, one hand behind her waist, the other between her shoulder blades.

"I thought successful stock ventures were your job before you found the Abbotts," he said. His voice rumbled nicely against her ear.

She felt herself relax. "My job, but not my life. And it was more about tracking their success and figuring out why it happened than the money earned from it. For me, though I'm sure my clients appreciated the money."

"I'm sure they did. But you're not planning to go back to it?"

"I doubt it. I'm thinking about a coffee bar."

"What?" He leaned back to stare at her face with an expression of astonishment.

"Don't worry. I understand you're adding a coffee shop. I'm just talking about a coffee *bar.* Mocha cappuccinos…"

"I know the difference," he said. "What I meant was, I cannot see you in a coffee bar."

"Why not?"

"Not enough things to take charge of, for one thing," he said. "Too few decisions involved. You stock various kinds of coffee, maybe some goodies, but the customer gets to make all the choices. You'd be bored stiff in two days."

She was offended. "You aren't."

"I have hundreds of products. I get to figure out what my customers want."

"Maybe I'd be really good at it."

"I've no doubt you'd be good at it. I just don't think you'd enjoy it."

"Well, shouldn't that be my concern?" She was getting huffy—inevitably. "And why are you worried about what I'm doing with my future if you don't want anything to do with me?"

"I didn't say I don't want anything to do with you."

"Yes, you did. You don't want anything to do with me *romantically.*" She said the word with quiet emphasis. "I have three brothers, a sister and two sisters-in-law if I require family advice on anything. What does that leave for you to do?"

"You don't need a friend?" he asked. It was a feeble reply, but he had to maintain some connection. He added on a jocular note, "I'll be staying in my new room tonight at your house. I'll be handy for advice or sympathy."

She thought a moment, obviously taken aback by the suggestion.

"No," she said, finally blowing air between her lips

in unladylike exasperation. "Excuse me," she said, then left him and went back to the table.

He helped himself to a glass of champagne from a passing waiter with a tray. This, he realized, was one of those "be careful what you wish for" moments. He'd wanted her to accept that there could be nothing between them. Now that she'd refused friendship, he had what he wanted.

Feeling the bleak reality of his request, he'd have happily changed his mind. But that wouldn't have been good for her.

He downed his champagne, and spotted Joe Fanelli carrying in a platter of strawberries dipped in chocolate. He looked very serious.

"How's it going, Joe?" he asked cheerfully when Joe saw him and came to offer him a berry. Joe hadn't been scheduled at the shop the past few days, but he was working for him tomorrow. It would be his first full day alone.

"Hanging together for now," Joe replied. "I'll take good care of the shop tomorrow, don't worry."

"I'm not worried."

"Good. Well, I'd better move on. Hope the wedding goes well."

"Thanks. See you Sunday."

"Come on, Brian." Campbell caught his arm and pulled him toward the table. "Fulio's carrying in the prime rib. We're going to need red meat to make it through tomorrow."

"Amen to that," he said, allowing himself to be led

back into the crowd. Campbell at least had a wedding night at the end of the long day.

FOUR HOURS LATER, Janet sat in the middle of her bed and brushed her hair, hoping the soothing strokes would release the tension in her, which was building into a headache. After her argument with Brian, she'd done her best to avoid him, but Campbell had brought him to the table when the main course arrived, and sat him directly opposite her and her mother.

She'd tried to ignore him, but he seemed determined to charm her mother and Tante Bijou and anyone else who would listen with stories about his college days with Cordie, who'd been at Columbia the same time he had. They'd worked in the drama department, he'd said, she creating costumes, and he making props—often weaponry for Shakespearean productions.

What Janet wouldn't give to run him through with a sharpened wooden sword right this minute. He was in his room in the new addition. Although it remained unfinished, her mother had had the bedroom set moved in so that he could stay with them tonight.

"I want all my family together," Chloe had insisted. Janet guessed that, considering all Chloe had suffered because of the kidnapping, she was allowed that passion for togetherness.

Normally Janet would be the last woman in the world to force herself on a man who wasn't interested in her, but every instinct told her that Brian was.

The house had grown quiet about half an hour ago and she felt fairly sure everyone had gone to sleep. Everyone but she, who couldn't seem to forget what it had been like to dance in Brian Girard's arms.

At the rap on her door, she looked up. "Yes?"

Her mother pushed her way into the room, a diaphanous underwater-green dressing gown fluttering at her ankles, a large book in her hands.

"I saw the light under your door," she said, coming to the bed. "I know you're troubled tonight."

When Janet shook her head to deny that, Chloe handed her a large scrapbook. "Don't lie to me, *chérie*. I saw it at dinner. You feel…disconnected?"

Janet put her brush down and touched the leather cover of the book. The Abbott name was embossed on it. She smiled up at her mother. "I do, but not from you. Not from the family."

Chloe framed Janet's face in her hands and leaned solicitously over her. "I know how strange it must be for you to be here. I appreciate that you gave up your old life to stay with us, to learn who we are and to teach us about you. So I've brought you a…a workbook, shall we say?"

She moved to sit beside her and opened the cover. "My Children" had been written in elegant script, followed by "beginning in 1979."

She pointed to a photo of two little boys in bathing trunks, a tall, handsome man standing proudly behind them in shorts, his shirt open to the wind. The boys held buckets and spades and sported big smiles.

Janet read the caption aloud, "Nathan with Killian and Sawyer," and smiled over the photograph. To see the two children and know the high-powered businessmen they'd become was fascinating. As was the photo of their father. She could discern the hard angles in his face, which Killian had today; the devilish grin that was so Sawyer; the restlessness about his windswept look that brought Campbell to mind.

There were many photographs of the boys, at birthday parties, in an apple tree—Killian standing proudly in a notch, Sawyer hanging upside down like a monkey. They were photographed with their father getting into the limousine, with Chloe in their Sunday best.

"That was my wedding suit," she said of the dusty-rose dress and jacket that showed off the slenderness of a much younger woman. "I won Sawyer right over," she said, her voice sounding wistful, "but Killian was a challenge. That's what makes him such a good businessman. He takes nothing for granted. Sawyer, on the other hand, has always been willing to take a risk."

Tucked in with the photos were report cards, awards for academics, ribbons for athletics.

"They were a couple of little geniuses," Janet said, admiring a first-place award for spelling bearing Killian's name in calligraphy.

"Yes, they were," Chloe agreed. "I've never spoken badly about their mother to them, but I can say this to you. She had to have been a heartless robot to just walk away from them."

She turned a page, to reveal Killian as a young teenager wearing a suit, Sawyer beside him, looking considerably younger, though only two years separated them. Killian had reached puberty, and Sawyer had yet to catch up. Campbell, a toddler, stood in front of them.

"Killian's grade-school graduation," she said. "He was already going to work with his father on weekends and breaks, fascinated by the business world. Nathan told me how fortunate he felt to have him, how safe he knew the family business would be in his care."

"It would be such a worry to have a child who didn't care," Janet agreed, "or couldn't cope. I mean, you'd want him to do what made him happy, but a business made up of people you care about is such a responsibility—particularly when it's been handed down to you by generations of your flesh and blood."

Chloe put an arm around her and squeezed her shoulders. "Your father would be so happy to know how well you understand that." She hugged Janet closer. Her smile was a little sad. "He would have died of missing you had I not reminded him that he had three other children who needed him very much. I so wish he could have seen you come home."

Tears filled Chloe's eyes. Janet was overwhelmed by the kindness and emotional generosity of her family, but there was a small empty space in the middle of the powerful joy. It was because she would never know her father, and had no memories of him.

"I study my brothers," she said, forcing cheer, "and can imagine a little of what he was like."

"He loved to rock you," she said, flipping pages until she found one depicting just that. Nathan sat in a wicker rocker on the porch, a baby in his arms wrapped in a blanket. "You weren't more than a couple of months old here," Chloe said. "He sang old Elvis songs to you. You were never a good sleeper. He paced the floor with you when your first two bottom teeth came in, and sang to you for hours."

Knowing that contributed to the feeling of being embraced she'd experienced from the moment she'd arrived at Shepherd's Knoll.

At the bottom of the page was a photograph of the three boys gathered around their father, looking down on the baby in his arms. "You charmed everyone with your first screech," Chloe said. Campbell was the only one you really annoyed when you began to crawl. Killian and Sawyer were old enough to remember to put their things out of your reach or understand that your reign of destruction really wasn't your fault."

Janet laughed at that term. "'Reign of destruction.' Killian said Campbell's always felt guilty because he'd been angry at me for breaking one of his trucks the day I was taken."

Chloe nodded. "He shouted for me very indignantly and I carried you out of his room. You adored him because he was nearer your age and had a lot of toys that appealed to you, too. He was a touchy child. He loved his brothers but was very different from them. Though we never differentiated between Susannah's children and my children, he was somehow aware of their brilliance and his less-dramatic talents. So he was always protecting what was his."

"Makes him a good estate manager," Janet said. "He was so on top of everything when Brian's father tried to destroy the house. And he was inspired to hire Winfield. Winfield couldn't care more about all of us if he was family."

Chloe nodded. "We're lucky to have such a wide range of talents in this house."

"I'm not contributing anything at this point," Janet said. "But I hope to rectify that soon."

"Take your time about that, Janby. You contribute so much by simply being here." Chloe got to her feet and kissed the top of her head. "I'll leave you to look through the album by yourself, but don't stay up too late. You don't want bags under your eyes when you walk down the aisle."

"Good night, *maman*."

As Chloe closed the door behind her, Janet went backward in the photo album to study the pictures Chloe had passed over in order to show the one of Janet and her father.

The house was now completely quiet. She smiled at the two older boys, Killian holding what must have been Campbell as a baby. He was younger than in the photo of his siblings and him gathered around their father and Janet on the porch.

There were more birthday parties, Chloe accompanying what appeared to be school field trips, several pages of photos taken in Europe when Campbell was a babe in arms.

Janet drank in the happiness on their faces, the obvious connection among them, even though the older boys were Susannah's. She realized her good fortune to be born into such a family.

Then there was a photograph of the boys with a tall, middle-aged woman, thick hipped and bosomy, a long gray braid hanging forward over one shoulder. Her smile was shy as she posed for the photograph, one hand on Killian's shoulder. He appeared to be about ten.

Something was curiously familiar about the woman, and Janet peered closer, wondering if she could recognize her as someone in the Abbotts' current lives. Unfortunately, as with many of the photos of Nathan, there was not enough detail.

The woman appeared in many of the photos that followed, always with the children, and Janet began to conclude that she was the nanny. Then Janet came upon a picture of the woman seated with the boys on the top step of the porch, Janet—or Abigail, then—in her lap.

At first glance, Janet was fascinated with the portrait of herself at that age, wide eyes, big smile, arms outstretched and reaching for the camera. The boys were all looking toward her and laughing. Even the nanny, who in all the other photos offered only a shy smile, was laughing.

The nanny.

Janet's eyes went back to the woman's face, clearer this time because of the proximity of the photographer—and stared in disbelief.

No. It couldn't be. The nanny was just another woman with similar features to those of the aunt who'd been so much a part of her and China's lives.

Heartbeat tripping, Janet turned on the bedside light and placed the album right under it, letting it illuminate as much as possible the nanny's face.

Her heartbeat began to accelerate. The woman could have been cloned from Janet and China's aunt Kate, who had been their adoptive mother's older sister, a woman even their mother acknowledged as a little odd and off center.

She'd been away from home for many years, apparently traveling the country to find something Janet's mother had never been able to define. She'd said she doubted even Kate could.

Peggy Grant had also said that a man had been responsible for Kate's eccentricity. She'd left Paloma in boredom at thirty-five, excited and happy to embark on a quest for adventure. She'd returned ten years later a changed woman.

Her adoptive mother had insisted that when Kate, five years older, had been a girl she'd been as normal as the next young woman, except that she'd been big boned and exaggeratedly curvaceous and the boys at school had teased her.

She'd started college, hoping to encounter a different experience, but it was the same there. She wasn't pretty and petite, so she was ignored or teased.

She'd left school before finishing her first year, worked for a bank for seventeen years, then visited one day to say she was tired of the tedium and was taking to the road.

"She'd write to me once in a while," Peggy had recounted. "And we'd commiserate—I because I couldn't get pregnant, and Kate because she couldn't find a man. They were all jobless or unfaithful or married. I told her to pick more carefully."

Janet's heart punched her in the ribs. "We'd commiserate—I because I couldn't get pregnant…"

Oh, my God! The words grew loud in Janet's head. *Oh, my God!* She wondered if she was looking at the face of the person who'd kidnapped her at fourteen months of age—to give her sister a baby.

But that was ridiculous! Janet forced herself to calm down, told herself she was being ridiculous, that this couldn't possibly be the same woman who'd been her aunt and died ten years ago of a sudden heart attack.

A lot of people looked alike. Wasn't there a saying about everyone having a double?

Janet might have been able to convince herself of that if the woman in question had not been involved at both ends of the twenty-five-year-old mystery surrounding Abigail Abbott's kidnapping. How likely was it that one woman would serve as nanny to a group of children, one of whom was taken, and that her double was the sister of the woman who'd adopted the abducted baby?

The air left Janet's lungs. Her heart was now pounding, and as anatomically backward as it seemed, she could feel it in her head.

She slipped the photo out from under the sealing sheet and into the pocket of her robe, left the book open to that page and scrambled to her feet, needing an answer to the unbelievable question. She had to find the photos she'd brought with her from home. Winfield, she remembered, had taken them up to the attic.

Maybe she wasn't remembering her aunt correctly. After all, ten years had passed.

She made her way quietly downstairs, through the dark kitchen, to the flashlight always kept by the back door. Then she climbed the long, narrow flight of stairs at the back of the house. She flipped on the light and a high-wattage bulb illuminated the sloped ceilings and everything under them.

She looked around for familiar boxes and spotted none. The room was filled with old furnishings, several trunks stacked to one side, skis propped in a corner, fishing poles balanced in a gun rack on the wall.

There were dozens of boxes, each neatly labeled with what it contained—boys' school papers, Nathan's decoys, fabric, Christmas ornaments and, in a far corner, a whole pyramid of boxes simply labeled "Susannah."

Then, near the trunks, Janet spotted the familiar boxes that had started her and China's searches—the very ordinary document boxes with their names on the lids that had led them in wrong directions at first, but eventually to their families.

She located the bright pink shoe box in which she'd kept family photos, intending for years to place them in an album as Chloe had done. Obviously, Chloe was far more organized than she was.

After pulling the box out from near the top of the stack, she held up her small flashlight and sifted through the photos, remembering a group shot taken the Christmas before her aunt had died. The whole family was in it. She had to see her own photo of Aunt Kate to prove to herself that she wasn't insane.

She found the photo and put the flashlight down so that she could study it. Her mother and her father, her mother and China, her father and China, her mother and Aunt Kate.

Janet picked it up, fingers trembling, and held the flashlight to the face of the woman standing arm in arm with her mother.

She had gray hair, though she wore it in a bun rather than in a braid, and had a distant look in her eye and a smile that didn't seem to belong on her face. That was precisely the way Janet remembered her—always loving to her sister, always bearing gifts and treats for her nieces but somehow never quite there.

That curious detachment was visible in this photograph.

She took Chloe's photo out of the pocket of her cotton robe and placed it beside the one of Aunt Kate. The faces were the same; she'd swear it. Only, something had happened to Aunt Kate in the intervening years. Something that had caused that strange withdrawal.

Janet shuddered. The woman had kidnapped her from the Abbotts and never forgiven herself.

She felt a desperate need to run. She didn't know why, she didn't know where to, she just needed speed. She kept her two incriminating photographs, then swept the others back into the box, dropped it on top of the stack of her things, flipped off the light and closed the door.

Then she ran down the stairs, a giant bubble of some unidentified emotion growing inside her, swelling with each step she cleared. She had to know what happened. She had to find out for her brothers, who'd borne guilt for her disappearance all these years.

There was an odd sound in her throat when she burst out of the dark stairway and into the kitchen. She stopped, because whatever was making the sound was hurting her throat. She was gasping—or sobbing. She had to regain control before she went upstairs. No one could know about this until *she* was sure.

The kitchen light went on suddenly and she was staring into Brian's face. He wore shorts and a T-shirt and held a coffee cup in his hand. His hair was tousled, his eyes concerned.

"Janet." He looked into her face, then put his cup down and pulled her toward a stool. "What the hell happened?"

Chapter Seven

"Janet," Brian said again, feeling her arms trembling under his hands. "What is it? Is someone up there?"

She opened her mouth to reply, but couldn't. Instead, she shook her head. Dry, apparently involuntary sobs were coming from deep inside her.

"No one's up there?" He wanted to confirm again.

She shook her head again.

She was starting to scare him. He'd come down for something to either wake him up completely so he'd stop dreaming of her, or put him to sleep so he'd stop thinking about her. He'd vacillated between coffee and brandy, and finally put them together.

He grasped her waist and lifted her onto the stool, then pulled another one up in front of her and sat. He took her hand and placed his cup in it. "Have a drink," he said. "I'm right here. Nothing's going to hurt you. Just take a drink." He pushed her hand toward her mouth to encourage her.

She drank, hesitantly at first; then, maybe getting the taste of alcohol in the coffee, she took a deeper sip.

She was still shaking and making those noises.

He encouraged her to sip more and she did. She closed her eyes and drew a breath, and he wondered if the brandy was beginning to make a warm spot in her stomach. It didn't stop the trembling, but it stopped the sobs.

"What were you doing in the attic?" he asked, smiling, hoping to get a smile out of her. "Did you see a mouse?"

"I…I…" She had a voice now, but was unable to form words with it. She handed him something clutched in her fingers.

He took it from her and saw that it was two photos, somewhat crumpled from her grip. He put them side by side on the bar, smoothing them out, and leaned over to study them. He recognized the Abbott nanny from years ago, with all the Abbott kids. She also appeared in a second photo, but he didn't know the woman with her. "Who am I looking at?" he asked. "The old nanny? But who's the woman with her in this Christmas picture?"

Janet cleared her throat and opened her mouth to speak. Her voice was quiet, but it was there. "The other woman is my adoptive mother. The woman you're calling the nanny was my aunt Kate."

He stared at her, confused. "The Abbotts' nanny was…your aunt Kate?"

She nodded vehemently.

"But you hadn't even been born when she was here. Wait." He stopped to rethink that, remembering that the nanny had been here when Abby was taken. She'd been questioned by the police, then cleared. "Right. She was here when you were a baby. When you were kidnapped." He still didn't get it. "I don't understand," he admitted.

"She was my aunt Kate," Janet said carefully, as though trying to understand it, too, "in my *other* life. She was—Peggy Grant's sister. China's and my aunt Kate."

He was silent a moment; then, his brain scrambled. He had to clarify her claim. "This woman—" he pointed to the picture of her with all the Abbott children "—who lived here and took care of your brother and you when you were a baby, lived in Southern California where you grew up?"

"Yes. She was there as far back as I can remember—as my mother's sister."

He looked at the pictures again, thinking that if he stared at them long enough, he'd find an explanation.

"Do you know the nanny's name?" she asked, her voice growing a little stronger.

He thought a moment but couldn't remember. Then he turned the photo over, hoping for identification, and there it was. "'Kate Bellows,'" he read aloud, "with Abby, ten months, Killian, eleven, Sawyer, nine, and Campbell, five. That's right. Kate Bellows."

"Kate Bellows," she said, putting both hands over her ears. "I feel like a gong is sounding over my head. "Kate Bellows was my aunt!"

He studied the photos one more time. The woman appeared to be the same person, yet not. "Are you thinking that *she* kidnapped you?" he asked.

Janet spread her hands helplessly. "Doesn't that seem

logical? She's the one connection to Shepherd's Knoll and Paloma, California, three thousand miles away. What else could it mean?"

"I don't know. I do remember, though, that the kids liked her a lot. And she had a lot of patience with them. She picked them up from school all the time, and Sawyer was always making her wait. He used to love the monkey bars and she'd finally have to go get him. She wasn't here very long."

"I thought you and the Abbotts hated each other when you were children."

"We did. Although my hatred was fueled by envy. They always looked so happy. Their father seemed to love them so much, and mine had no use for me at all. I used to wait to be picked up, too, so I'd see her come for them. I was a little young, but the story is that the police questioned everyone in the house at the time and still couldn't find reason to suspect anyone in particular."

"Don't you think this suggests she had something to do with it?"

He had to agree. "So, what do you want to do?"

"Can I have another sip of that?" she asked, pointing to his coffee.

He handed it to her, then went to pour himself another cup. He left the brandy out this time, though. He had a feeling he was going to need his wits about him.

She took a sip, then appeared to be measuring him. She was beginning to adjust to what she'd learned, was looking like her old self again.

"I'm not going to tell anyone about this," she said

firmly. She put her cup down. "We behave throughout the wedding as though nothing's happened."

"Ah. We? My services are requested?"

"Can you deal with that," she asked, folding her arms, "if I promise not to try to seduce you? You offered to be my friend."

Proximity to her was dangerous for him whether she came on to him or not. She just had to be there.

"Sure." After he spoke, he wished he'd gotten more details, but it probably wouldn't have mattered. He'd have done whatever she asked anyway. "What's involved?" he questioned her belatedly.

She seemed to be thinking a plan through as they spoke. "My mother—my adoptive mother—always told China and me that she and Daddy adopted us through the family doctor. Well, that turned out to be true in China's case, but not in mine. Still, he might know something about it."

That sounded logical. Brian guessed the next step. "You're going to Los Angeles to talk to him."

"Yes."

"A simple phone call won't do?"

"It's harder to lie to someone face-to-face. I'll tell the family I've sold some property there or something and I'm going back to sign papers. I'll leave the minute China and Campbell are off on their honeymoon."

"You'll get some flack from Chloe."

She smiled wryly. "Not if I explain that you're coming with me. Not only will she not be worried about me taking off on my own, but she likes the idea of you and me. She'll send me off with her blessing."

"So I'm going along as bodyguard?"

He could tell by the tilt of Janet's chin that she'd completely recovered from her shock. "That appears to be the only role you're willing to fill. You'll be relieved to know that I've taken several self-defense classes. You can just stand by and watch."

He rolled his eyes. "A little full of ourselves, aren't we?"

"I've been rejected by Losthampton's most eligible bachelor, now that Campbell's getting married. I have to do something to pump up my self-esteem."

"You were redirected," he said, taking the point of her chin in his hand. "Not rejected."

She put her hand to his, held it there for a moment, then drew it away. "Funny," she finally said. "Felt the same. See you at the altar."

She stood to leave, and it was as though the ground opened and prepared to swallow him—after chewing him first. No way could he let her go to bed after that shocking discovery, thinking that he was keeping his distance from her because he wanted to.

He caught her arm, pulled her back to him and kissed her the way he'd wanted to every time he'd seen her. He felt her stiff surprise, her gradual relaxation against him, then her arms wrapping around his middle and holding on.

He explored her mouth, nibbled her jaw, her earlobe, the cord that ran to her shoulder. He slipped a hand under the back of her shirt and pressed her closer, his hand splayed between her shoulder blades. He dipped his hand lower, letting her feel the evidence that rejection was the furthest thing from his mind.

She squirmed uncertainly—a moment he found both torturous and delicious—then settled in his embrace as though she belonged.

"I did not reject you," he said into her ear, then planted a kiss on her jaw.

"Good." There was urgency in her voice as her breath puffed against his ear. "Because I could really use your help."

"You have it."

She was silent a moment but continued to hold him tightly. "This doesn't feel like friendship."

"You told me you didn't want me for a friend."

She sighed against him, then leaned back to look into his eyes. Hers were confused, uncertain. "Then... what are you offering?"

"Me," he replied. "And I'd say the less we analyze it, the better. I'll book us on a flight to L.A. Sunday morning."

That didn't clarify anything for her, but it did bring a frail smile. "Thank you," she said. She patted his chest in a gesture of gratitude, then picked up her photos and left the room with a parting smile for him over her shoulder.

His heart melted and his manhood turned to iron.

Okay. It was a dichotomy he was getting used to when dealing with her.

THE WEDDINGS of Sawyer and Sophie, and Campbell and China, were the most beautiful Janet had ever witnessed. The brides were lovely and so clearly happy, and all the Abbott men with Brian beside them were an impressive picture.

The press had clamored around them on the church steps, but Winfield had hired a security team to help him keep them outside.

In the church, the atmosphere was spiritual and joyous. Janet felt great happiness for China, even while she knew her sister's marriage would change their relationship forever. China was now committed to a husband, and though he was Janet's brother, their alliance would have to claim space that had once belonged to her.

Janet was fine with that, of course, though a little melancholy.

Sophie's children were beautiful as they walked her up the aisle to give her away. Little well-dressed clones of their usually tumbled and sandy selves. Gracie, ten years old, and her six-year-old sister, Emma, wore lavender-flowered dresses and tea roses in their hair. Eddie, eight, walked with uncharacteristic gravity in a miniature tuxedo. He gave his mother's hand to Sawyer, then he and the girls joined China's father in the pew Chloe occupied. The careful plans that had gone into the events of the day were perfectly executed.

Janet held last night's surprising discovery close to her, smiling through the ceremony and the reception afterward in the gardens of Shepherd's Knoll. But seeing her siblings resplendent in their formal dress made her more determined than ever to find answers to the questions surrounding her kidnapping. She wanted to be able to tell her brothers exactly what had happened, and to prove to them once and for all that they bore no guilt in it—even a child's self-inflicted guilt.

Her mother approached her at the buffet table. "Janby, what's going on?" she asked. She was chic in a tunic and asymmetrical skirt, the shade somewhere between pink and purple. "You look as though you should be wielding a sword and shield, as though you've made up your mind about something." She studied Janet as one of the catering staff placed a butterflied shrimp on her plate. "Tell me you're not leaving us."

"I'm not leaving you," Janet replied dutifully, holding her plate out for shrimp. Then she noticed the coconut-dipped shrimp and asked for one of those, too. "At least, not for very long. I got a call this morning that a property I owned in Malibu sold. I'm going back in the morning to sign the papers and make sure everything's in order. It should take only a couple of days." She smiled at Chloe and met her gaze, hoping she wouldn't suspect her daughter had just lied through her teeth.

Chloe seemed suspicious, then worried. "I don't like you flying off by yourself all that way," she said. "Yes, you're perfectly capable and lived a whole life on your own before we found you, but I can't help it. I died a little when you and China went home to close out your apartments."

"Then you'll be happy to know," she said, helping herself to a delicious fruit kabob and putting one on her mother's plate, "that I'm not going alone. Brian's coming with me."

Chloe's eyes widened in surprise, then a bright smile made the worried look disappear. "At last! That antagonism between a man and a woman is often a sign of attraction to which neither wants to admit."

"He's coming as my friend," Chloe told her with what she hoped was convincing nonchalance. She wasn't sure herself what he considered his status after that kiss; she only knew what *she* wanted. "Now that he has someone to watch the shop, it's easier for him to get away."

"Well." There was a wealth of hope in the simple word. "That makes me feel much better. How long will you be gone?"

"I'm not sure. I may show him around a little while we're there. But probably by next weekend."

"We're going to have a big empty house next week, with two couples honeymooning, Killian off to London and you and Brian in L.A. If not for Sophie's children, Cordie and I'd be rattling around here like a couple of spinsters."

"Let Cordie handle Sophie's children," Janet advised. "She needs the experience. Her twins will be here before you know it."

Chloe smiled at the prospect. "That's true enough." Her eyes suddenly brimmed with emotion. "It's hard for me to remember that just four or five months ago I had three brooding sons and a missing daughter, and now I have three deliriously happy sons, a charming extra son in the bargain, my daughter restored to me and five grandchildren! How wonderful is that?"

"Pretty wonderful." Janet was amazed by how much her own life had changed.

If she could solve the mystery of who'd kidnapped her, Janet thought, she could give something back to the family who'd welcomed her so warmly.

Brian appeared at her side with three glasses of champagne, two held carefully in the same hand. "Follow me before I drop these," he said to Janet and Chloe. "It's standing room only on the lawn, but I saved you the old bench in the garden."

"How did you save it if you're here?" Chloe asked.

"I have cohorts," he replied. "I bought them off with the promise of extra wedding cake."

"With all the people who came," Janet said, "I hope you can pay off."

They started to move from the buffet table.

"Ohh." The exclamation of surprise and delight came when the bench was in sight—and occupied by Gracie, Eddie and Emma. Eddie leaped off the bench at the sight of Brian, leading his companions.

"I'm glad Mom got married to Sawyer," he said, "but I can't believe I have to spend the last Saturday before school starts again in this suit!" He pulled at the collar of his shirt.

"But you are so handsome." Chloe leaned down to kiss his cheek. "Thank you for saving the bench for us."

"Brian said we could split his cake and Janby's."

Janet made a face at Brian as she sat on the bench. "By whose authority did you give away my cake?"

"I assumed you'd be happy to do it," he explained,

handing her one of the glasses, then Chloe. He went to lean against a nearby stone garden lantern and sip at his own, "To be able to sit down with your food."

"Okay this time," she said, winking at the children, "but you'll have a shortened lifespan if you go around bargaining with my desserts."

Eddie pointed to her plate. "I didn't see any of that fruit-on-a-stick stuff when I got my food."

"They just put it out." She pointed her fork toward the table. "Go get some."

The two younger children ran off toward the food. "Are you going to try to catch the bridal bouquet?" Gracie asked Janet, squeezing in between her and Chloe. "If you do, you'll be the next one to get married. 'Cause now you're the only one in the family who isn't."

"You're not married," Janet teased her. "Mom's not married."

"That's right!" Gracie turned to Chloe. "Grandma, you can try to catch the bouquet. But who would you marry? I mean, there isn't anybody around who's…you know…older."

Chloe put her fork down and pinched Gracie's chin. "For your information, if I ever plan to get married again, I'll look for a younger man."

"Wow, Grandma."

"Yeah. Wow, Mom," Janet added. "I didn't know you'd given this thought."

"Why not?" Chloe nibbled on a shrimp, her eyes speculative under the brim of her hat. "I think a nice young man who likes to travel and dance and who appreciates big families would be perfect for me."

"I think you're right," Brian said. "We'll have to find someone for you."

"Thank you," she said with a demure tip of her hat, "but I'd like to find him myself. Yes, Gracie," she said to the little girl. "Janet and I are both going to try for the bouquet."

"I'll go tell Mom to aim it at you," she said, running off, presumably to do just that.

A short time later, the cakes were cut and served. Janet, getting another cup of coffee for Tante Bijou, was surprised when Brian appeared beside her again, this time holding a plate with cake on it.

"Here's some cake to go with that coffee," he said, trying to hand it to her.

She resisted. "This is Tante Bijou's coffee. And I thought you bargained away my cake to the children."

"When you threatened my life over it, I gave them Campbell's cake, instead. This is yours."

There was a large ivory-frosting rose on it. "Yum," she said.

She delivered Tante Bijou's coffee just as Cordie brought her a slice of cake. Cordie put a hand to her round stomach and rolled her eyes. "These babies are very lively this afternoon. I don't think they want me to eat any more beef-and-blue-cheese roll-ups."

Janet grimaced. "I don't think I want you to do that, either. Are you okay? Do you need to sit down?"

"You want me to get Killian?" Brian asked.

"No, thank you. I'm fine. I'm going inside to put my feet up."

As Cordie waddled away, Janet took a bite of cake. It was delicious. "Mmm. This is so *good!*" she said to Brian. "Have a bite."

He shook his head. "But thanks. Our flight leaves just after three tomorrow. We'll get in a little late, but I thought that was better than having to get to the airport at some ungodly hour."

"That's perfect. You're sure you want to come with me?"

She prayed he hadn't changed his mind. He'd been attentive all day, but he hadn't mentioned what had happened last night. She was afraid the impact of that kiss, even though it had all been his doing—well, most of it—had made him change his mind.

"I'm sure." His eyes were steady on her face, their message difficult to decipher. They watched her boldly but told her nothing. "I was going to drive, but Daniel said your mother asked him to take us."

He pointed with his coffee cup to the limousine as Daniel pulled it into the driveway. Killian and Sawyer came out of the house with bags that had been piled in the foyer since early that morning.

"Excuse me. I'd better go lend a hand." Brian loped up the steps and went into the house. He returned a moment later with a bag under each arm, Campbell following with more.

By the time they were finished, everyone had gathered around, waiting for the bouquet-throwing ritual.

Chloe hooked an arm in Janet's and marched with her to the middle of the group.

"This is our chance, *ma chère*," she said. "We must not be shy."

Sophie and China stood side by side on the porch, having changed into traveling clothes for the ride to the airport and their separate destinations.

Janet saw her brothers and Brian leaning against the limo's trunk to watch the action. The boys noticed their mother in the lineup and looked at one another in wonderment.

Sophie turned her back to the group, and while they cheered encouragement, she tossed the bouquet over her head. As though Queen Elizabeth of England herself was trying to catch it, the crowd parted as Chloe raised her hands toward the flowers. She caught the bouquet by the ribbons with one hand, to tumultuous applause. She looked surprised and delighted. Then, realizing everyone had given her the field, she still held it to her, clearly happy to have caught it under any circumstances.

The women collected again as China turned, preparing to throw her bouquet. She swung a little awkwardly; it hit the pot of hanging fuchsia on the porch ceiling and tipped toward the limousine.

Brian instinctively reached out a hand and snagged it.

There was deafening applause again and the suggestion from one disappointed young woman that China toss it once more.

"No," China said. "It falls where it falls. Brian's the next one to get married."

There was more applause and several photographers closed in to get pictures. There was backslapping and hooting from Killian, Sawyer and Campbell.

Birdseed was thrown, hugs were exchanged and the two couples climbed into the back of the limousine. Janet, who'd had very little time today to talk privately with her sister, saw her blow her a kiss through the window, her eyes telling her she was sorry, too, that they'd missed a chance to speak.

Knowing China was going to be deliriously happy, Janet blew the kiss back and waved cheerfully as the limo drove away.

The crowd began to disperse. Janet stayed by her mother and Killian as they sent guests on their way.

It seemed hours later that Janet walked into her bedroom. In a corner was the bag she'd packed, and on the dresser sat a few things she wanted to make sure to throw into her purse in the morning.

But she ignored everything and simply fell onto her bed on her back, physically and emotionally exhausted.

She uttered a little cry of alarm when her cheek connected with something both soft but prickly on her pillow. She leaned up on an elbow.

It was the bouquet Brian had caught, with a note attached: "Since I have no plans to marry, I thought I'd pass this on to you."

Chapter Eight

It was after nine in the evening at Long Beach International Airport and the temperature was still in the high nineties. Brian led the way across the vast parking lot, heading for their rental car. He carried two bags, and Janet followed, dragging her tote. Blessedly, there was no humidity, but he missed Losthampton's coastal breeze. The smells of diesel fuel and hot pavement filled air that felt as though it hadn't stirred in generations.

Brian found the car, a small silver mid-size, popped the trunk with the remote and put his bags in. He turned to take the tote from Janet and saw that she looked worse than he felt. The flight had been a long one with no food and little leg room. She'd only picked at the salad she'd bought in the terminal at O'Hare, where their flight connected to its second leg after a three-hour wait, and she'd stirred restlessly in her seat most of the way.

He wondered if she was afraid of what they might discover—or that they might hit a dead end and learn nothing. He'd tried to talk to her about it, but she'd an-

swered in monosyllables and pretended interest in the
in-flight magazine to fend off further discussion.

She'd looked hot and tired and completely miserable when they finally landed at the Long Beach airport.

"We'll get a cold drink before we get onto the freeway," he promised. "You know where we're going?"

"Yes. I made reservations at a motel just a couple of
blocks from where China and I grew up. The doctor's office building was just a few blocks away. I'll give you
directions." She gave him a tepid smile. "I'd offer to
drive, but I'm so sleepy. I'll just back-seat drive, instead."

"Whatever will get us there. How far are we from a
shower and dinner?"

"At least an hour," she said forlornly.

Brian had been to Southern California on business
for the November Corporation many times, and the free-
ways amazed him. Drivers moved at seventy miles an
hour with only half a car length between them. Driving
toward Paloma tonight reminded him of how happy he
was to be living in a small town on Long Island a mere
ten minutes from his store.

His life had undergone an enormous change, but he
thought he was beginning to get his feet.

As he drove, he looked around him at the six lanes
of traffic, the semitruck in the lane beside him, the high-
rises all around and realized he wouldn't have come here
by choice—only by the request of Abigail/Janet
Grant/Abbott.

God. He was falling in love with her. He remembered
watching her across the altar during the wedding, see-

ing her glossy hair embroidered with flowers, her dark eyes glistening as her sister repeated her vows. She was so full of love for China, and for her rediscovered family and anything and everything in its orbit. And she was attracted to him, heaven knows why.

He couldn't imagine anything that could mean more trouble for both of them than the desire to be together. Life would be forever reminding her of his feckless mother and his vengeful father.

He'd been so sure that he couldn't let this happen— and yet he was doing it. The wit and beauty in her face tended to make him forget his resolve to keep his distance. And when she looked into his eyes with lust and longing, he was lost.

The fact that she needed him now destroyed whatever distance from her he'd managed to maintain. And it hadn't been much anyway, after that kiss.

She directed him expertly, giving him plenty of warning for changing lanes or making turns. It was hard for him to think of her as a veteran freeway fighter.

"Do you miss this?" he asked as he got off the freeway and followed the traffic to a broad boulevard.

"Right turn here," she said. "No. I loved it here when I lived here, but now that I've had a taste of small-town life, I don't think I could come back."

"You don't miss the excitement, the pressure?"

"No." She turned slightly in her seat to watch him. "Do you?"

"I don't," he admitted, "but sometimes I feel guilty that I'm enjoying my shop so much, and my grandmother's house. I think I should be doing something more worthwhile, something that benefits other people."

"You provide the products that keep vacationers comfortable and happy," she said. "That's worthwhile. Men and women who finally get a break from the kind of job you used to have enjoy time to recharge themselves, time for their children and their friends. And you keep them supplied with things they need. How many fathers and sons have rented boats from you and gone off to spend a great day together?"

That might be a slightly naive picture of his work, but he liked that she thought of it that way. And it gave him a new perspective on it.

"Where are you going to put this coffee bar you have in mind?" he asked, determined to be more supportive of the idea than he'd been when she first brought it up.

"I'm still scouting out locations."

"Where?"

"Not in town," she said, "because there are a couple already. Somewhere on the beach, I guess. Not too big. Cozy." She pointed ahead and warned, "Keep an eye out—the motel's just a block or two away."

Seconds later, he turned into the parking lot of a sprawling, two-story motel with Polynesian-style architecture from the sixties. The office had been built to resemble a hut, and above it was a colorful neon sign of a Polynesian totem. Tiki Town. *Vacancies* flashed on and off.

Brian pulled into the parking spot under a canopy in front of the office, then slanted a grin at Janet as he stopped.

"Yes, I know." She forestalled comment by opening her door. "Cheesy. But when I was surfing the net for places to stay, I recognized the name and remembered it was just blocks from my old home and the doctor's office."

He hurried around the car to help her out. "I wasn't going to criticize. It's very retro, and that's always in style."

A large, cheerful Latino man greeted them at the desk. Janet registered and was given two key cards. "Second floor," the man said, "other end of the building. Enjoy your stay."

"I can take my own bag," Janet insisted after Brian had moved the car.

He was going to remind her that she had to climb stairs with it, but she was already walking away. He intercepted her about five steps from the top. She was now dragging the bag up one stair at a time.

He passed her, opened the door to one of the rooms, then went back to help her up the last few steps.

"How can cotton summer clothes be so heavy?" he asked, carrying her bag into the room.

"Blow-dryer," she said wearily, following him, "travel iron, book to read…"

He put her bag down near the bed at the same moment she sank onto the edge of a beige coverlet patterned with palm trees. "You brought an iron?" he asked in disbelief.

"It's just a travel iron," she said, letting herself fall onto her back. "Oh, Brian. I cannot tell you how good this feels. Only a shower is going to feel better."

He had a suspicion dinner was no longer an option tonight. A shower would relax rather than revitalize her.

"Want me to find some takeout while you're showering?"

"Ice cream sounds good." She stretched her arms and closed her eyes. "And maybe a cup of tea. Would you look in the bathroom and see if there's a coffeepot?"

There was. "And coffee and tea."

"Great. I'll make that while you're gone."

"You're sure all you want is ice cream? You haven't had much to eat today."

"I'm too tired to eat more than that."

"Okay. I'll see what I can find."

She pointed languidly up the street. "There used to be a little market and gas station about a block that way. Open-all-night kind of thing."

"Okay. Don't fall asleep until I'm back with your ice cream."

"Don't be long."

He put his things in the room next door, then headed off up the street.

He was back to his room in ten minutes with a gourmet ice-cream bar for Janet and a ham-and-cheese sandwich for himself. He rapped on her door, half expecting Janet would still be in the shower or already asleep.

But she pulled it open, wearing a light cotton robe and a towel around her head. Her face was free of make-up and touchingly young. She reminded him of the morning she'd fallen off his dock. He squashed the impulse to take her in his arms and make her forget all the things that troubled her.

She swapped the ice-cream bar he offered her for a cup of coffee.

NOTHING COULD HAVE made Janet happier at that moment than a vanilla ice-cream bar covered with buttercrunch pieces.

"So, the store's still there," she said.

"Yeah. Great little place. Reminds me of mine."

"What did you get to eat?"

"Ham-and-cheese. Thanks for the coffee."

She wanted to invite him into her room, but she was too tired to be rejected. Even though he insisted he hadn't rejected her. Since that kiss the night before the wedding, he hadn't touched her or even mentioned what had passed between them.

She knew why. Their relationship was too complicated. Too difficult to try to predict what could result from it. And who needed that when she was trying to figure out who was responsible for changing the whole course of her life.

She took a step back into her room. "Well, I'll let you get some rest. Thanks for going for this. Breakfast is on me."

"Sure." His eyes went over her face with that bold look that suggested things he never put into action. She concluded she was reading things into his gaze that weren't really there.

But just in case.

"If I knock on the wall, will you knock back?"

It was a moment before he replied. "Yes," he said finally. "Are you afraid?"

She denied that with a shake of her head. "Just...a little lonely. Shepherd's Knoll is so filled with activity and I've gotten used to that. It's so quiet here."

"Yes. Well. Call if you need something." He walked away from the door and she closed it, then went to bed with her ice-cream bar and cup of tea.

Delicious, she thought, but a sorry substitute for what she really wanted in her bed.

THE FOLLOWING MORNING, Brian pulled the rental car up to a modest ranch-style house in a quiet neighborhood lined with jacaranda trees. It was white stucco, with a red barrel-tiled roof and an arched entrance. She noticed a tricycle parked in the middle of the small lawn.

"This was my parents' house," she said. She and China had stopped to look at it when they'd closed up their apartments and talked about how strange one's sense of time was when emotions were high. It felt as though they'd walked out the front door to college only yesterday, and that had been almost a decade ago. Yet now, Janet's life with the Abbotts made her last visit seem like an eternity ago, though she'd been with them less than two months.

"It's a pretty little place," Brian said, leaning forward to see around her.

She smiled, strong memories stirring her of all the love that had filled the house. "I was happy there."

He patted her knee companionably. "Good for you. I grew up in a mansion where everyone was unhappy. Ready to go? If you want to be at the medical office by ten…"

The clock on the dash said ten minutes to ten.

"Yes, I'm ready," she said. As Brian pulled away, Janet saw a sturdy little boy about four burst out the front door and race to the trike. She liked that as her last image of her family home.

Eight minutes later, Brian drove into the large lot behind a three-story office building landscaped with small trees and birds-of-paradise.

"You're sure your old family doctor still has an office here?" he asked as he opened her door.

She shook her head, scanning the building. "I don't think so. I tried to find him on the Internet and couldn't bring up his name. But I located this office complex, and there's a doctor in his old space."

"You're thinking he might know where your doctor is?"

"It's a long shot, but I thought if I got here and looked around, I'd be more likely to find him than if I'd kept searching blindly online."

"Okay." He put a hand on her shoulder, the first time he'd touched her since the kiss. "Let's give it a try."

She leaned into him and looped an arm around his waist, liking the comfort of being so close to him. "I'm glad you came with me," she said.

He squeezed her shoulder. "Otherwise you'd have had to go in search of that ice-cream bar yourself."

He stopped to open a glass door for her, but she ignored the shadowy interior of the building. "You know that isn't why I'm glad."

"Yes." His expression was grave. "I know it isn't."

She socked his arm playfully. "Then please lighten up about it, okay? Trust me. Nothing's going to happen between us if you don't want it to, so let's just enjoy the moment. We're on an adventure together." She shook her head. "Well, maybe not an adventure. More like a reality search. Whatever happens, happens. I'm a big girl."

He pinched her chin. "And you're my best friends' little sister. I value my life." He pushed her gently into the hallway.

The interior of the building was cool and dark. She stopped a moment to let her eyes adjust. "Your life would be in danger only if you broke my heart," she said, smiling. "And if I'm resigned to just taking my chances..."

He led her around a stairwell, through a door and into a more brightly lit corridor. A door opened in a bank of elevators.

"Third floor," she said, drawing him in with her and pressing the button. "We're looking for Dr. James Goodson's office."

They found a floor directory near the elevator when they walked off, and followed the corridor until they located the office number. The fresh-faced receptionist in Dr. Goodson's office had been there only a year, and didn't know whether he'd bought old Dr. Chandler's practice. She asked Janet and Brian to have a seat, and said she'd try to catch Dr. Goodson between patients to see if he could squeeze in a moment to talk to them.

The waiting room was filled with people of all ages, many of them coughing and sneezing. Goodson had a big day ahead of him.

Janet settled in one of two chairs in the middle, willing to risk a cold or the flu to get answers to her question.

"You can wait in the car, if you want," she said to Brian, who sat in a chair beside her. She added quietly, "Doesn't sound like this is the healthiest place to be."

"I'll stay," he replied quietly, "but I'd advise you not to touch the magazines."

"Right. Oh, hi."

A toddler walked unsteadily toward her with a wide smile, very soupy eyes and both arms raised for balance. When she was within a foot of Janet, she wobbled dangerously and was about to fall on a thick pad of diapers. Janet instinctively caught her hand to steady her.

The baby laughed and raised her other arm in the classic "pick me up" signal. Janet complied, and settled her on her knee.

"Oh, I'm sorry!" A young woman with a screaming baby in her arms came from across the room. "Livvie is very sociable! I was so busy trying to quiet the baby so he wouldn't drive everyone else insane that I didn't realize she was bothering you."

"Please don't apologize," Janet said. "And she's not bothering me. How old is she?"

"Thirteen months. I'm afraid she's probably very germy. I brought the baby in for his regular checkup, but I was hoping the doctor could do something for Livvie, too."

Livvie crawled over Janet and into Brian's lap. Janet

was a little surprised when he reacted calmly, offering the toddler a hand to hold when she stood up on his knees, wobbling. Her other hand had a death grip on his hair.

"Oh, jeez," her mother said while the baby continued to wail. "My husband's in Iraq and she really misses him."

"Donna Cunningham!" a nurse called from a door into the examining rooms.

"Oh, that's me!" The young mother held the baby to her shoulder and tried to catch Livvie's hand. Livvie screamed and held tightly to Brian's hair. "Livvie, we have to go see the doctor."

"No!" Livvie said firmly, both arms now wrapped around Brian's head.

Janet tried to disengage them, but the child began to scream.

"How about if I follow you to the door," Brian suggested, holding Livvie close and standing up. Livvie stopped screaming and smiled into his face. Then she smacked his nose.

Donna Cunningham headed for the nurse and Brian followed, Livvie sitting happily on his arm. Transferring her to the nurse's arms started another round of screaming, but by then they were inside the corridor. Brian closed the door as he came out.

He resumed his seat beside Janet. "I suggested you not touch the magazines, but it didn't occur to me to tell you not to touch the babies."

Janet laughed. "She was so cute. She seemed to have a thing for you." She smoothed his hair where the baby had disturbed it. It was thick and wiry.

"I'm generally irresistible to women."

"And very good with babies."

"It's hard not to like them."

"You realize," she said, "that this puts you in a whole new light."

"How's that?"

"Well, before, you were simply tall, blond and handsome. Kind and very appealing to me in a way I don't really understand and can't describe."

He didn't seem to know whether to be flattered or worried. "And that's changed?"

She leaned an elbow on his shoulder in the tight confines of the chairs and felt a firm resolve forming inside her. He was not escaping her.

"Yes. Now maternal instinct has kicked in. When I dream about my future children, you're the man I'll see by my side because you were calm and patient and very sweet with Livvie."

"She had me by the hair," he reminded her. "I had little choice."

"Actually, you did." She leaned closer to plant a gentle kiss on his lips, unmindful of the other patients in the waiting room. "You could have withdrawn from her, put her on the floor, asked her mother or me to take her. But you didn't. You behaved like perfect father material."

"I'm not."

"You are." She kissed him again. "I'm sorry, Brian, but you're the man of my dreams. Before I saw you with Livvie, I'd have accepted your insistence that you can't get serious about me because of the threat you present to my reputation." She smiled over that. "I don't believe a word of it, but I was coming to the conclusion that there must be something else inside you holding you back, maybe something even you don't understand, and I should honor that." She shrugged all that away. "But I've changed my mind. Men who'd make good fathers as well as good husbands are so few and far between that you're dead meat, buster. Your heart is mine."

Chapter Nine

Brian was very grateful when the nurse called Janet's name. He followed Janet in, and the nurse led them to a narrow cubicle where a man in a lab coat sat making urgent notes on a clipboard. He appeared to be in his middle thirties, his face young, though he had gray hair at his temples.

He glanced up at them and raised his pen in silence, obviously asking for one more minute.

He scribbled a few more lines, then put his pen down and got to his feet. "I understand you're looking for Dr. Chandler," he said.

Janet nodded. "He was my family's doctor when I was a child," she said, her voice a little high. "I thought that since you were in the same office, you might have taken over his practice."

He shook his head. "No, I didn't. When I came here from Oregon, the office was already vacant. I think his patients were transferred to Dan Guttierez on Bellrose."

Brian saw Janet's shoulders fall.

"Are you trying to find information on one of his patients?" the doctor asked.

Janet nodded. "I need to know something about…about my family, and I thought he might remember."

"You should talk to Greg Lattimer," he said, "in the insurance office across the hall. He's been in the building for ten years and is always telling me stories about their poker games. He'd know where Chandler is."

Brian followed in Janet's wake as she hurried excitedly out of the office and across the wide corridor to the door bearing the Greg Lattimer, Inimitable Insurance sign.

Lattimer was just on his way out to coffee when the receptionist intercepted him. Janet explained that she wanted to find Dr. Chandler.

Lattimer was very short, very round and very eager to help. He turned to the receptionist. "Look him up on the client database, Chelsea," he said. "Chandler, Arthur. We always exchange Christmas cards."

With the stroke of a few keys, she had the address, printed it out and handed it to Janet.

Janet studied it in surprise. "Thank you," she said to Lattimer. "I expected it to be more difficult than that."

"Nothing's difficult at Inimitable Insurance. You two sure you have enough coverage? You have children yet? They should be covered, because you…"

Fortunately, the friend he was meeting for coffee came to see what was holding him up and Janet and Brian took the opportunity to escape.

"Where is the good doctor?" Brian asked as they rode down in the elevator.

"Desert Haven Senior Living," she said warily, probably expecting Brian to protest. "Palm Springs."

"Palm Springs," he repeated. "Maybe we should call first and make sure he's still there. Do you have the number, too?"

She was already dialing her cell phone.

"Hello," she said after a moment, then stopped. *Answering machine,* she mouthed at him. Then she said, "Hello, Dr. Chandler, this is Janet Grant. I don't know if you remember me, but you took care of my family and me in Paloma until I was a teenager. I'm in the area, and would love to stop by and say hello and…talk." She looked doubtfully at Brian when she added that last, inadequate word. Then she left her cell-phone number, turned off the phone and dropped it in her purse.

"He sounds very lively," she said, her eyes bright. "His message lists his daily activities and the times in between when he can be reached. So if I want to catch him between golf and social events, I have to visit before noon."

"If he's that busy," Brian said, "he must be in good mental health and have a good memory."

She'd obviously drawn the same conclusion. "Isn't that great? Come on!" She grabbed Brian's arm and pulled him toward the car. "We can drive down this afternoon, stay the night—and be at Desert Haven first thing in the morning. Okay?"

"Okay."

"I'm sorry to drag you all over the place."

"It's all right. I'm resigned to being your slave for the duration of this trip."

She grinned as they climbed into the car. "Really? I didn't know you provided anything other than driving services. Does that mean you'll fill my bathtub and brush my hair?"

Those sounded like duties he'd happily undertake. But he couldn't make it that easy. "I'd have to know that, ultimately, there's liberation in it for me. That I can buy my own freedom."

She considered him, several complicated emotions chasing across her eyes. "Good try, but not a chance. I'll draw my own bath and brush my own hair. You're destined to be the father of my children, Brian. No freedom for you, I'm afraid." She snapped her seat belt into place. "Can you find us a Krispy Kreme? I'm starving."

BRIAN WAS QUIET for most of the drive south. Janet wanted to think that was because the traffic was fairly heavy and he was concentrating on the road, but she was sure she'd be deluding herself.

"You're wondering how to fend me off, aren't you?" she asked when they had slowed to a crawl. "We can talk about it. I'll listen to your arguments."

"I wasn't thinking that at all," he replied. She turned to him in surprise. The traffic had stopped completely and he met her gaze. Then his eyes went slowly over her face, feature by feature. "Actually," he said, "I was planning a seduction."

She stared at him, stunned. "Of…me?"

"Of you. I'm even willing to risk your brothers' vengeance."

She was now caught off guard and completely flustered. "You mean…you finally see what I see?"

His brow furrowed. "I'm not sure. What do you see?"

"You and me in a cozy old house, a couple of children and a little dog from the animal shelter." She smiled hopefully. "Is that at all close?"

He shook his head. Her heart sank.

"I see a big dog from the animal shelter," he corrected. "No vows, no kids, at least until we're sure it'll work."

She wasn't sure she liked the sound of that. Still, it was something. "Is anyone ever sure?"

The traffic began to move and he focused his attention to it. When it finally smoothed out, he answered her. "I suppose not, but we have a little more to worry about. Do you want your children to have a grandfather who's in lockup in a hospital or in jail, and a sordid history on their grandmother's side?"

"I want them to be confident in the love of their parents. And to have the devotion of doting aunts and uncles. I think we have that part sewn up."

"That's true. But this press-pestering life we live will always be with us. What if we had a son who dreamed of running for office, or a daughter who fell in love with the son of a senator? Don't think for a minute that everything in my history won't come up to haunt them."

That didn't upset her a fraction as much as it did him, but she wanted to be understanding of his concerns.

"Okay," she said, "but…you were planning a seduction. You must be thinking there's a way to work it out."

"I'm thinking you should decide if it's worth it to you to take the chance."

She was filled with disbelief and disappointment. "You mean test-drive you," she asked, "to see if you're a good enough lover for me to involve emotion and promises?"

He shot her a surprised glance. "No," he denied. "I—"

She cut him off. "If that's your idea of seduction—"

"I meant," he interrupted angrily, "that you're an impulsive woman who likes to have what she wants. And since your whole lifetime is involved here, you should take the time to make sure I'm really it."

"I *was* sure," she said, folding her arms and leaning her head back, eyes closed, "until you started hedging your bets."

"I'm hedging *your* bets."

"I'm used to assuming my own risks, thank you very much. Just look out for yourself. Which you seem to be doing."

"Mmm. That must be why I let you haul me across the country."

A tense silence stood between them the rest of the trip. It was dusk when they reached Palm Springs. Tall palm trees wrapped in sparkling lights flanked Palm Canyon Drive, and elegant storefronts offered the wares only the very rich could afford. That was her now, Janet realized, though she was so poor in spirit at the moment, financial wealth had little significance for her. Still, she could appreciate the beauty of Palm Spring's main thoroughfare.

Thinking they should find a place to stay that was not too far from the Desert Haven, she reminded Brian stiffly that it was on Calle Caliente.

He ignored her.

"If you want to find a place near—"

"I know where I'm going," he returned sharply.

"Ah. Do you mind sharing that with me?"

He gave her a glance that could have felled a redwood. "You're supposed to be a woman used to taking risks. Just wait and see."

Fortunately, she was angry enough herself to deflect his look with one of her own. "I thought that since we were doing this together—"

"We're not doing it *together*," he contradicted her. "*You're* doing it, and I was invited to come along and conform. Relax. I made reservations while you were having your third doughnut. I promise it'll be at least as charming as Tiki Town."

She fumed silently as he drove most of the way through town, then turned onto a side road and drove a half mile more before a subtly lit, sprawling hotel became visible in the encroaching darkness. It had been built to resemble a Mediterranean villa and boasted a scripted neon sign that said it was the Palm Palace.

As Brian pulled up in front, a portly young bellman hurried out, rolling a luggage rack. Brian popped the trunk and the young man pulled their bags out and placed them on the rack. A parking attendant helped Janet out of the car, then took the keys Brian handed him.

"Mr. Girard!" he said in surprise, then frowned at the car. "What happened to the Porsche?"

Brian offered his hand. "Hey, Jake. Changed my life and changed my car."

"I see," Jake said, his eyes going over Janet once with a sort of respect. "Are you in the November Corporation's suite?"

"No."

"The bridal suite?"

"No. I asked for one of the bungalows around the small pool." Brian introduced Janet. "She's not my bride, Jake, but a young lady I'm helping with an investigation."

Janet was surprised by the young man's friendly attitude toward Brian. She'd had no idea Brian was familiar with Palm Springs and he'd said nothing on the drive about knowing where to stay. She wondered with a strange mixture of annoyance and guilt if this was the seduction he'd had in mind.

She often forgot that he'd traveled on business for his father for years before he was disowned and had abandoned that life for the general store and boat rental.

Jake gave her a courtly bow. "My pleasure, Miss Abbott. I hope you enjoy your stay. And find what you're looking for."

Well, that was clearly not going to happen, but she smiled politely in return. "I'm sure I will. Thank you, Jake."

Jake gestured the bellman forward. "This is Luís," he said. "He'll take good care of you. And I'll put your car in the usual spot. See you, Mr. Girard."

"Thanks, Jake." Brian led the way inside and Luís brought up the rear with the luggage rack.

"Hello, Judith," Brian said to an attractive desk clerk who handed him something to sign.

"Hey, there, Mr. Girard. Saw you coming and have everything ready." Then she noticed Janet. "Hello." She spoke brightly, her eyes going to Janet's hair. "Can I make you a salon appointment? Do you need a massage? A spa treatment?"

Janet wasn't sure if she was being helpful or critical.

"Thanks," Brian replied for her. "We're here for a very short stay. Lead on, Luís."

The bellman walked them out a side door and along a lit, flower-lined path to one of several bungalows built around a swimming pool. If that was the "small" pool, Janet thought, the other must have its own tides.

Luís stepped aside to let Brian open the door, then followed them inside and drew the cart into a bedroom.

The living area was the size of Shepherd's Knoll's living room, and had a fireplace, a bar, several conversation areas; it wandered into a sort of cabana room with French doors that went out to the pool.

There was also a fully equipped kitchen, and a sumptuous bedroom that had a fireplace.

Brian gave Luís a bill, thanked him and walked him to the door. He held it open until the cart was clear. She wondered if he'd used this bungalow before. He seemed very much at home in it.

He went directly into the bedroom, then returned with his bag and put it in the cabana room. She watched his angry movements, regretting their argument, though not her position in it. She also felt badly that he'd made reservations at this wonderful place and now all they could do here was glower at each other.

"You've stayed here before?" she asked conversationally as he crossed to the bar.

He dropped ice cubes into a barrel glass. "The company has a suite here."

"I heard that. But I mean, this bungalow."

"I've played in golf tournaments here for charity." He poured Scotch over the ice. "This is a nice quiet place to be that doesn't make me feel like I'm here on business."

"I didn't know you knew Palm Springs," she said. She'd intended that admission to precede an apology, but changed her mind when he replied.

"I thought you knew all there is to know about me, including my innermost thoughts and intentions."

"All right, maybe I misunderstood you," she said, moving around him, careful not to touch him, to study the lineup of bottles. "But how else was I to take what you suggested?"

"The way you've been coming on to me," he said, moving his arm out of the way when she reached for a bottle of Muller-Thurgau, "I thought you *wanted* to make love."

"I do!" She splashed the wine into a tulip glass until it was almost full. "I was thrilled that you were thinking about seduction."

"Then what in the hell…?"

"You made it sound like I was conducting an experiment."

"Well, isn't that what spending time together is?"

"Spending time together might be, but making love should happen *after* you're sure you're with someone you want forever. How making love is for us wouldn't determine how I feel about you."

"It would affect how you feel. Good sex makes you want more."

They'd moved into the middle of the living area, neither one of them apparently relaxed enough to sit down. Brian leaned a shoulder against one of two columns that separated the bar from the rest of the room, and Janet paced around a large sofa, gesturing with her wineglass.

"Good sex can develop from caring," she argued. "Emotional compatibility is there or it isn't. I don't care how good the sex is."

"And you've experienced this yourself?" he challenged.

"My fiancé changed his mind weeks before our wedding," she replied, her voice quieting, her chin firming. "The sex was good, but we disagreed on where to live and when to have children. I wanted to stay in L.A. because China was here, and our father was old. And I wanted to have a baby right away. He wanted to move to Oregon and raise grapes. The work was hard, he said, and there wouldn't be time for a family right away. Our arguments about it always ended in lovemaking. I thought he'd come to agree with me, but apparently not. He left. So the sex ultimately didn't really figure into it."

Brian studied his glass, then reached behind him to place it on the bar. "I'd say if he was your first lover, you might not have been able to judge how good the sex was. But chances are you've had others since."

Though he hadn't phrased it as a question, she thought it was. She sat on the sofa and took a big drink of wine. "No," she admitted finally. "That failure scared me. It didn't put me off men, or anything, but it made me want to analyze a relationship more closely before I gave my heart, my dreams away. I kept looking for the right man, but I never felt that connection again…until you."

"Now that China's in Losthampton, you'll want to stay there?"

"I don't know." She took another sip of wine. "That was three years ago. Our parents are both gone now, China has Campbell and my life has completely changed." She tossed her hair and said firmly, "But I still want the baby."

Brian knew that. "Yes," he said. "I saw you with Livvie. And with Sophie's children."

"So, if we're fighting about this," she said, leaning back into the sofa, swirling the contents of her glass, "you must have had a different experience. Lots of lovers, I suppose, being rich and handsome?"

He couldn't quite believe they were having this conversation. He went to sit on the sofa opposite the one she occupied. "Not as many lately," he said with a candor that surprised even him, "as when I was young and thought I had a lot to prove."

"And those relationships were just about sex?"

He considered that a minute and finally said, "In all honesty, they didn't even qualify as relationships. Some of the women were impressed with my money. Some had their own money and were intrigued with my bad-boy image."

She seemed surprised. "You had a bad-boy image? You're so solid and responsible."

He wasn't sure whether to be pleased or offended. "My father hated me. I loved the business, but he didn't trust me to know what I was doing and gave me only small responsibilities. I drank too much and acted like a jerk. My only real friend in the world at that time was Cordie."

She sat up in surprise. "Cordie? I heard you went to school together, but I didn't realize…"

"I loved her," he said, wanting to divulge the worst, "but she was wild about Killian from the moment they met."

She put a hand to her heart. "You *loved* her?"

"I did. And in those days, as I've said, the Abbott brothers and I hated each other. We had roughly the same amount of money, but apart from that, they had everything else—loving family, good friends, good reputations, and I had nothing."

She leaned toward him, her arms crossed on her knees.

"There was an incident in Paris," he went on, "when Cordie and I were there for the fashion shows. She was buying for Abbott Mills, and I was marketing for the November Stores. She was married to Killian."

Her eyes widened, but she waited for him to go on.

"We'd switched rooms in the hotel because her door didn't lock. It was late and we were all tired. A short time after we switched rooms, I realized I'd kept the second key, so I took it back to her. She didn't answer, so I let myself in and put it on her bedside table. Unfortunately, Killian had gone to Paris to surprise her and walked into her room at the same moment."

"Oh, my God."

"Yeah. For reasons of his own, he was willing to believe she was fooling around with me. And for my own selfish reasons, I was willing to let him."

"Brian!"

"I told you there was a lot you didn't know about me."

"But…I can't imagine Killian would believe that of Cordie."

"It's complicated," he said on a sigh. "Has a lot to do with you, actually. For most of his life after you were kidnapped, he wouldn't let himself have fun. He thought if he hadn't left that night and gone to a friend's party, he'd have intercepted whoever abducted you. He grew into a very serious man with nothing but work on his mind. Then fun-loving Cordie walked into his life and changed everything. He was swept away by her, they got married quickly, then a few months later he woke up to realize that the anniversary of your abduction had come and gone and he hadn't even tortured himself about you. He sent her away because she'd made him have fun and forget about you."

Janet put both hands to her mouth. "No!" she said. The sound came out muffled.

"She eventually brought him around. I became an honorary Abbott when I helped save Sawyer, and they're all living happily ever after. Except you and me. And I *want* you to be happy."

He thought he had her there. He'd revealed the devious machinations of his mind and his cruelty to her brother. If anything would discourage her from loving him…

She lowered both hands to her lap, entwined her fingers and asked quietly, "Then, what if I have to have *you* to be happy?"

Chapter Ten

Brian couldn't determine what had gone wrong there. Unless it was that Janet was involved, and that seemed to make every plan he'd conceived work against the outcome he'd planned.

As he struggled to answer that, she stood and went to put her wineglass on the bar. Then she came back to him and sat on the edge of the coffee table. He could see the gold flecks in the depths of her eyes, the silken texture of her skin, caught her complex floral scent.

"Would it convince you of my seriousness," she asked, her expression sincere, "if I suggested we test your theory?"

That took him completely by surprise. He opened his mouth to issue a quick affirmative but didn't seem able to say it.

"I know men and women approach the whole thing from different points of view," she said, putting a hand on his. "Maybe for a man, making love tells you more than it tells a woman. I mean, all we learn is that a man is good in bed, and that doesn't necessarily translate to good on his feet. But a woman takes all her emotions to bed with her. It's possible it would tell you something I—"

"No," he said. And then he said it again, because he wasn't sure he'd heard himself the first time. "No. It was just a bad idea. I'm sticking with my original stand that it's just all too messy for us to ever have anything together."

She looked as surprised as he felt. "Messy?" she asked at last.

He wasn't sure what he meant, except that she had his emotions and his libido tied in a knot and he had no idea what he wanted anymore. "My history, your complicated views on everything. I'm with you until we figure out who took you from your family, then I'm sticking to my neck of the woods and you'd better stick to yours."

She stared at him in disbelief, then her eyelashes fluttered like a sign her brain was trying to compute what he'd said. "But we share the same *neck of the woods*. My family is your family, as well. We live in the same small town. Don't you think this is something we should resolve?"

Making love to her would have been such an easy solution. He was sure he could have conveyed the depth of his feelings for her, the tenderness and passion that were all scrambled inside so that when he touched her, he never knew which would surface.

He wouldn't make love to her now because, as he thought that through, he realized that meant he was thinking with the wrong part of his anatomy. She was being so honest; it wouldn't be fair.

"Let's just go to bed," he said finally, pointing to the bedroom as he got to his feet. "You in there, and me in the cabana room. I'll call for breakfast at seven, and you can be at the doctor's place as soon as he's available to visitors."

"Okay." She stood, too, looking as if she'd just been punched and hadn't regained her bearings. "Good night." She walked around him into the bedroom and closed the door.

He usually slept in his underwear but had brought a pair of cotton pajamas in deference to her presence. He put the bottoms on, then pushed the French doors open and inhaled the wildflower fragrance of the high-desert night.

He'd hoped the fresh air would revive his spirits, but the smell of flowers reminded him of Janet. He left the doors open and lay on the sofa, trying not to remember that he'd just squashed her like a bug. But had he not done that instantly and firmly, he'd have taken advantage of her offer. And he was sure that once he'd had her, he'd never be able to let her go.

She wouldn't be able to stride into her future while shackled by all the old Susannah Abbott-Corbin Girard history.

He closed his eyes, convinced she'd thank him one day. It was little comfort.

He woke up after eight and scrambled out of bed, to find her dressed and on the phone. She put a hand over the receiver and asked amiably, "Bacon or sausage?"

She was placing the breakfast order he was supposed to have attended to an hour ago. "Bacon," he replied.

"Portuguese sweet bread or marmalade muffin?"

"Sweet bread. Black coffee."

He heard her repeat his order as he gathered up his things.

"Fifteen minutes," she said, hanging up the phone. "Shower's all yours. I'll get the paper."

She wore a simple white pants outfit this morning, and her hair was a glossy, tumbled cap. She seemed the epitome of cool—a fact that annoyed and confused him after the mostly sleepless night he'd had. He'd finally fallen asleep about five in the morning, physically and emotionally exhausted.

He turned on the shower and was nearly blasted into the opposite wall of the stall. If this was the setting Janet had chosen this morning, no wonder she seemed so calm. She'd been beaten into submission.

He pulled on beige slacks, a beige-and-brown cotton shirt, and light leather boat shoes.

Breakfast was on the table when he got there, both plates still covered. Janet appeared engrossed in the paper.

"You didn't have to wait for me," he admonished, taking his chair. She folded the paper aside and reached for the coffeepot. "Good manners should always apply," she said with unsettling courtesy. Then she poured coffee into his cup.

"Thank you." He was determined to match her mood despite the messy feeling that still prevailed. "Have you called Dr. Chandler?"

"He returned my call." She poured her own coffee.

"He remembers me! He said to come any time after nine. Apparently, he does calisthenics from eight to eight forty-five."

She spread apricot jam on the toasted sweet bread. "I don't think I've ever had Portuguese bread."

"It's one of the restaurant's specialties. Has a cardamom flavor."

He waited while she took a bite. She closed her eyes and made a sound of approval. "Mmm. That's marvelous."

"I'll bet Kezia would make it for you if you asked her."

"If she won't, you'll just have to find a bakery that makes it and stock it in your store." She looked at him over their food, a hint of the anger she had to be feeling toward him flickering in her eyes. "I will be able to still shop there? Or is that out of my neck of the woods?"

"Janet…" he scolded.

She raised a hand to stop him. "I'm sorry. Here you go." She passed him the jam, then put the newspaper beside him. "In case you want to know what's going on in the world. I've been so wrapped up in my own issues that home could be another planet."

He could agree with that. This entire trip—spending time with her, sleeping with her just feet away from him, having her open her soul to him—made him feel like an alien to himself.

He'd been trying not to think too deeply about the past; instead, to concentrate on the here and now, to figure out where he was going and aim himself there. But she was always delving into things, exploring murky corners, shining light into areas he'd have been happy to leave dark.

He couldn't wait until she saw Dr. Chandler. He hoped the man could answer all her questions so that they could go home. At least he could put a mile between Janet and him on Long Island.

"Have you called your mom?" he asked her.

She nodded, pouring more coffee. "She lost Emma yesterday afternoon, but found her in a tree with Versace. Eddie came home from school with a bloody nose, and Gracie is waiting on Cordie, who's feeling a little under the weather."

"Oh-oh." He put the paper down. "She's not due until next month, is she?"

"No, but twins are often early. Mom's theory is that it's just because it's very humid and everyone's uncomfortable." She gave him a "So there" bob of her head and added, "You should be grateful that I've dragged you to a nice *dry* climate."

"Very considerate of you," he praised, but watched her as she focused on her breakfast, and he thought that in spite of everything, he wouldn't have missed this time with her.

DESERT HAVEN WAS a series of upscale, elegantly designed and decorated fourplexes scattered over several beautiful acres. In a large building that was the centerpiece of the landscape, there was a common room, a gym, a clinic and the administrative offices.

She followed the directions the doctor had given her when he'd called earlier, and found him easily. Janet recognized him the moment he opened the door. His hair had gone white and his face was lined, but otherwise he looked like the same man who'd set her broken arm when she'd fallen off her bike, administered shots of various descriptions and generally had kept her family healthy for as long as she could remember.

"Janet!" He wrapped her in a hug. "What a nice surprise!" He gestured her inside and shook hands with Brian as Brian followed her in and introduced himself.

The doctor pointed them to a brown leather sofa in a room filled with oak built-ins, family photos and a view of rolling acres and wildflowers.

"What a beautiful place!" Janet said, admiring the view before sitting down. "Your family had a weekend place in Palm Springs, didn't they?"

Dr. Chandler sat in a rocker that faced the sofa, where Brian joined Janet.

"Desert Hot Springs," he corrected her with a smile. "We retired there and spent all our time golfing and swimming. Does your family still live in Paloma?"

"No." She was surprised to feel a pinch of emotion. The past month she'd been so focused on the Abbotts that she'd had little time to think about the Grants. "My mother died a few years ago, and my father just passed away."

"I'm sorry," he said. "My wife died about a year ago. That's when I moved here. I hate to keep house, and I don't cook worth a damn, so this is the perfect setup for me." His grim expression changed to an accepting smile. "I've made a lot of new friends, the kids visit when they can, and I'm keeping up my golf game. You can't ask for more than that, given the way things have to change."

Janet nodded at his philosophy. "You're absolutely right."

He studied her, obviously remembering. "Now, there were two of you girls. Both adopted."

"That's right. You arranged for our adoptions."

She eyed him, half expecting him to deny that.

But he smiled, nodding. "My friend Dean MacDonald, an obstetrician from Canada, sent your sister to me. Your mother was so excited. She and your father had been trying to have a baby for so long."

Janet nodded. "That was China."

"Yes, it was!" he said with a light laugh. "Had you asked me to recall her name, I'd have probably said Paris. I recall she was named after some exotic location. Your mother said she got it out of a book or something."

Janet folded her hands together tightly. "Dr. Chandler, do you recollect how I came to you?"

He shook his head. "You didn't."

She'd suspected that, but if that was true, she thought a little desperately, where did she go from here? All she could do was tell him what she knew, to see if it matched information he had.

"My parents always told us," she said, her voice sounding strained, "that you brought us to them."

He shook his head again. Firmly. "That's certainly true of China. I remember that very clearly. Never saw a woman as excited as your mother."

Janet felt all her hopes of discovering the truth melt away in the heat of the morning. She turned to Brian and saw sympathy in his eyes. He put an arm around her shoulders.

"But you took care of Janet when she was a child?" Brian prodded.

"That I did. As I recall, the girls had all the childhood diseases, a couple of broken bones…"

"How old was Janet when you started seeing her?" he asked.

"Just a little over a year," he said. "'Bout the same age China was. Her mother said God answered her prayers twice."

Janet's breath caught in her throat. She had to force it to form words. "Then where did I come from, Dr. Chandler?"

"You mean they never told you? Even after you were grown?"

"No, they didn't." She braced herself.

The doctor looked horrified, as though reluctant to say.

Janet pleaded. "I have to know. And my parents are both gone, so it isn't going to offend or upset them. How did I come to them?"

He cleared his throat, then said quietly, "Why, you're your mother's sister's child."

She took in that information with a start. So that had been Kate's story. "I've had a DNA test," she said. "I'm the missing child of a family in New York."

The doctor frowned. "I don't know much about DNA testing. It's new technology since I was practicing."

She explained briefly about the boxes she and China had found, about the newspaper clippings that had eventually led Janet to Long Island.

"I don't know the answer," he said gently. "A couple of weeks after I took China to your parents, your mother brought you to me for a checkup. She said you were her sister's baby out of wedlock, and her sister couldn't raise you anymore, so she sent you to her through a friend. She even had a signed letter from your aunt to that effect. I encouraged your mother to make it legal, but she didn't think it was necessary."

She was too confused to form questions.

"If it's any comfort," he added, "she was just as excited about you. I asked her if she was sure she could cope with a second baby of about the same age, and she laughed. That's when she said God must have forgotten he'd answered her prayers and done it again. After all those years of being childless, she thought it was a miracle to have two such beautiful babies."

Her mind a muddle, Janet thanked the doctor. Brian shook hands with him again, and the doctor saw them to the door.

"I don't know what your search is all about," Chandler said, walking them to the car. "Just remember that you two girls were loved. It isn't everybody that gets that. You hear all the time about the most god-awful things happening to helpless children. But they gave you everything they could. And they loved you."

Janet hugged him. "I've always known that. Thank you, Doctor."

Chandler waved them off. Brian drove to the gates of the facility, then pulled off the road and turned to Janet.

"I'm sure the test was right," he said. "You can't be your aunt's child."

She'd never fainted in her life, but she felt as though she could just collapse right there in the maze that was her life and be lost forever.

"Could my aunt have had an affair with Nathan Abbott?" she asked.

"No." Brian put a hand to her cheek. "You were tested against Chloe. Chloe's your mother. And Nathan Abbott worked too hard to fool around with anybody. Your family says that Campbell's smile is just like his, and yours reminds me of Campbell's."

She caught Brian's hand, needing something steady in her personal turbulence. "Of course. I'm not thinking straight. Then, does that mean Aunt Kate just stole me from the Abbotts so her sister could have a baby?"

"Maybe. She might not have known the doctor had already found China."

She gasped. "I can't believe my parents would have taken a stolen baby, no matter how much they liked the idea of another child."

"It's possible your aunt really did tell them it was her baby, knowing they wouldn't have kept you otherwise. Maybe they thought she hadn't wanted to tell them she'd had a baby out of wedlock, then the baby became old enough to be a lot of trouble and need things she couldn't provide. So it seemed logical to them that she sent you to them when you were fourteen months old and needed someone to take you off her hands."

Facts and suspicion were spinning around in Janet's beleaguered brain. She looked fretfully at Brian, hoping he had an answer for this, too. "If my parents didn't know I was stolen," she asked, feeling sick, "why…did they keep the clippings about my kidnapping?"

He considered a moment with the calm calculation that sometimes drove her crazy but that she now appreciated. "This is just a guess," he finally replied, "but what if it was your aunt who saved them? You said she died a while ago."

Janet nodded, liking this so far. "I was sixteen."

"Okay. Did your mom clean out her place the way you and China closed up your parents' house?"

She didn't have to think about it, because she could still remember Peggy Grant's grief when she'd come home. Peggy had always been philosophical about her restless sister when Kate had been alive, but with Kate's passing, Peggy seemed to regret all they hadn't been able to share.

Then the very thing Brian was suggesting occurred to her as he said the words. "I'd say your mother found the clippings in your aunt's place and put it all together. You were sixteen, though, and there was no way she was going to part with you—even to soothe another mother's mind. But she left them for you, so that one day you could find your way home."

Janet put both hands over her mouth as she imagined her adoptive mother's pain.

Brian wrapped his arms around her and let her cry.

"We'll go back to the hotel," he said when she finally quieted. She rested her head back and closed her eyes. "You should sit in a hot tub, try to relax. We can decide what to do later."

"I have to find out exactly what happened," she said numbly.

"You have to accept that it may be a mystery you'll never solve. We'll keep trying, but your aunt isn't here to tell you why or how she did it."

"There has to be a way. This is the contribution I can make to the Abbotts."

"They're just so happy to have you back."

"I know. But if I can relieve my brothers of their guilt, I'll feel I've earned my place."

BRIAN DROVE back to the hotel, aware that he wasn't going to talk her out of making herself crazy until she solved the mystery of her kidnapping.

He ran a hot bath for her, found lavender and chamomile-scented stuff to put in it and called room service for two mimosas. He could use one himself. He had an idea, and he could only imagine what it would mean to the next few days of his life.

When the drinks arrived, he knocked on the bathroom door.

"Yes?" she asked.

"Place the bubbles strategically," he said, "I'm coming in."

Though she'd followed his instructions, she seemed

less upset by his presence at her bath than he'd expected. He handed her a glass.

"Orange juice?" she asked.

"Mimosa," he replied. "Nothing perks up good old
orange juice like champagne." He sat on the bath mat
near the sunken tub and clinked his glass to hers. "I had
a thought," he said.

"What's that?"

"Your mother said that a man had made your aunt Kate
funny. Did she have any boyfriends that you remember?"

"Never. She didn't even have women friends. Just the
family."

"Then," he said slowly, making sure his conclusion
was sequential to the facts, "the man must have entered
your aunt's life when she worked at Shepherd's Knoll."

Janet's eyes were unfocused as she mentally followed Brian's logic. Then she sat up abruptly, dislodg-
ing the concealing bubbles. She didn't seem to notice.

"That's true!" she exclaimed. "Why didn't I see that?
That makes so much sense!"

He had to focus on her face instead of the two beautiful little breasts now visible to him. "My mind's probably clearer than yours is at the moment." That wasn't
true, but it sounded good.

He caught a glimpse of her flat stomach and the inviting darkness below as she swung a curvaceous hip to
readjust her body. She rested her forearms on the side
of the tub to look at his eyes. Her eyes were excited but
worried. Again, he had to concentrate on them.

"How will we find out who it was? Chloe might

know, but I don't want to ask her. She'll wonder why I want to know, and I'll have to explain. I can't tell the family about it until I can present it as a solution—all questions answered."

"I have a customer who lives on a boat and does private detective work. I'm sure he'll help us."

She rested her chin on her hands, still holding on to the side of the tub. "Do you think it'll work?"

"I'm sure," he replied honestly. "We'll just keep trying until we're out of ideas."

She looked at him with adoration in her eyes. After the quarrelsome past few days, that surprised him.

She reached out a wet hand to touch his arm. "Thank you for helping me. I know it's been hard for you. I appreciate you, even when I don't agree with you."

"We agree that we care about each other." He couldn't take his eyes off the expression in hers, felt it draw him in. "We just don't agree on what to do about it."

She downed the last of her mimosa and placed the glass on the edge of the tub. She levered herself on her forearms until she could reach his lips with hers.

"I did things your way last night," she reminded him, "and you changed your mind."

He was getting drunk on that look in her eyes. "You can't imagine how much I've regretted that," he said, gently returning the kiss.

"Then why did you do it?"

"Because once I make love to you," he admitted, drowning in her as completely as if she were holding his head underwater, "I won't be able to think about protecting you from gossip and torrid news stories. I'll just want to keep you."

A sunny, satisfied smile formed on her lips. "That leaves me with only one course of action," she said before she kissed him again.

"What's that?" he asked against her mouth.

She touched his lips with the tip of her tongue. "Change it back."

Chapter Eleven

He didn't take much convincing.

Janet now understood that he loved her as deeply as she loved him, and put everything into making him see things her way.

She kissed him eagerly, thoroughly, her wet body drenching his shirtfront as he leaned down to accommodate her.

"Are you coming in?" she whispered, "or am I coming out?"

"Water's getting cold," he said, pulling her from the tub with an arm around her waist. He yanked a towel off the rack and wrapped her in it, then flipped on the heat lamp. "And you should really think—"

She kissed him again to stop him from going on, then unfastened the towel and handed it to him. "Just help me dry off, please?"

"Janet, that's not a good…"

She stopped him this time by wrapping her damp body around him. "Either that, or I'll dry myself against you."

"All right!" He lifted her away from him, picked up

the towel and turned her around. He dabbed halfheart-
edly across her shoulders, swiped once over her hip,
then swore and tossed the towel.

"I don't have a condom," he said. "We shouldn't..."

"Top drawer, beside the table." She grinned. "The
hotel is very thoughtful."

He carried her off to the bedroom, put her on her feet
on the plush carpet, grabbed a fistful of coverlet and
sheet and drew it back.

She helped him remove his shirt, feeling triumphant
at his desperate hurry. He dispensed with pants and
briefs with great efficiency, then all eager movement
stopped. He caught her arm, pulled her into his embrace, and she felt his sigh as they stood body to body.

"You've done it now, Janet," he whispered against her
hair. "There's no going back."

She tightened her grip on his waist and kissed the col-
larbone under her lips. "That's good, because we should
be concentrating on this moment."

He held her to him, placed a knee on the bed and lay
her on her back in the middle of the mattress. He knelt
astride her and kissed her eyelids, her lips, her chin,
traced a straight line of kisses down to her navel, then
returned to revere the breasts he'd missed on his
straight path.

She stroked the strong legs on either side of her, ran her
hands up his rib cage, then over his muscled shoulders.
Quicly, she helped him slip on the condom.

He held her to him and reached tenderly inside her.
She'd always thought that touch, even from a lover, a

sort of invasion, and her body's first reaction to it was always reluctance. But not this time. His touch, sure and possessive, changed her reluctance to eagerness as the pleasure spiral quickly began its work.

BRIAN FELT something change in her. She'd been generous and warm, but he'd felt almost a withdrawal when he'd reached inside her. He moved gently, and her response was instant. He realized that the good sex she'd talked about having with her fiancé had probably not been as good as she'd thought.

Proving the difference to her required little effort on his part because his body reacted to hers as though destiny had brought them together.

When her breathing quickened and she fretted against him, he rolled onto his back, taking her with him, and entered her. She made a small sound of satisfaction and began moving with the rhythmic spin that was claiming both of them. They rode it together in diminishing circles until she leaned backward in the throes of satisfaction, her body's little shudders generating his.

He caught her fingers in his to offer balance and she held on as pleasure overwhelmed him, as well.

It was a few minutes before she collapsed against his shoulder, whispering his name. He wrapped his arms around her and lay still, feeling her heartbeat against him, her arms wrapping tightly around him, and knew with sudden clarity that was what it was like to belong to someone, heart and soul.

JANET COULDN'T GET close enough. Now that she'd made love with him, she felt the utter tenderness that lived inside him and the intensity of his passion for her. It was as though they should share the same skin, breathe each other's oxygen. She wanted the certainty that nothing could ever separate them.

Then she realized with smug satisfaction that she knew it in her heart, and that was all that mattered.

"You were right about my having nothing to compare against Ed's lovemaking," she said. "What I had with him was very…I don't know. Ordinary, I guess."

"Well, let's face it." He drew the sheet up over them and tucked it around her shoulder. "There's nothing ordinary about us."

"He always seemed to have a good time, and that was what I enjoyed, I think. The fact that I gave him pleasure." She propped up on an arm to look down into Brian's face. "But he never made me feel the way you… made me feel."

He held her hair out of her face. "And how was that?"

"There isn't a word for it." She caught his hand and kissed its palm. "I felt," she said finally, "the way a diamond looks. All those places in the depths of it that you don't know are there at first glance."

He kissed her soundly and brought her back to him. "That's a beautiful way to put it. You made me wonder why I didn't listen to you the first time you told me we belong together."

Life was good. The past could hurt them only if they allowed it.

"But," he said, "we have to go home to finish this search."

She nodded reluctantly. That was the only smudge on her perfect horizon. "But I don't want the family to know what I'm doing until I can give them all the answers."

"You can hide out at my place," he suggested. "You'll have to keep a low profile because Losthampton's a small town. If anybody sees you…"

"You mean your grandmother's house?"

"Yes."

She levered herself up enough to plant a kiss on his lips. "I'd love that. I hope if we can find my aunt's boyfriend, or whatever he was, that he's still alive. My aunt would now be in her early sixties. If he was older…" She let that thought trail away worriedly.

"We'll follow this as far as we can," he said, kissing her, "but if we get to where we can't go anymore, you have to accept that we did what we could. And you know who took you—you just don't know why. That might have to do."

She leaned into him again, unwilling for him to see in her eyes that it *wouldn't* do. She *had* to know why.

THEY FLEW HOME the following day and drove through Losthampton in a rented car.

Brian privately thought Janet's family would not be as traumatized by the investigation as she was sure they would be, but she was determined and he was happy to have her close.

"We'll go in from the back," he said, taking a side road off the highway. It was after eight o'clock. "Bushes conceal the rear of my place from the road, so no one will know we're home."

"But you won't be able to go to the store," she reminded him.

"Not a problem," he said. "Joe's happy for the extra hours."

They skulked in under cover of darkness. He went to reach for the light switch in the kitchen, but she stayed his hand. "Someone will see the lights."

"I have a housekeeper who fits me in when she can and sometimes that's at night. They'll think it's her. Just stay away from the windows." He grinned. "She's about three times your size."

She wandered through the downstairs as he checked his answering machine and sorted through the mail.

"How fabulous!" she exclaimed, touching one of ten glass, lily-shaped shades on a tabletop lamp. Sculpted lily pads decorated the base. "Is this...Tiffany?"

"Yeah. It's signed."

"Good Lord!"

"Yeah, that's a lot of my problem with the place. I want it to be livable, but I suppose some things should be donated to the historical society and other things sold or given away. There's so much clutter, and we do need a few amenities."

She looked around at the relatively organized clutter. "Your housekeeper does a good job."

"She also keeps the fridge stocked and the place

dusted and vacuumed, but she says she just works around the stuff she's afraid to touch."

Deciding there was nothing in mail or messages that needed his immediate attention, he picked up their bags. Janet took her tote from under his arm and followed him upstairs.

He pointed to the large room his grandmother had occupied on one side of the house. "If you'd like your own room while you're here," he said, indicating it with a jut of his chin, "that one's spacious, has a large wardrobe and a television."

She smiled in surprise. "A television? The lady who had all that precious old stuff downstairs had a television in her bedroom?"

"She loved game shows. She didn't go to college, but prided herself on her knowledge of trivia."

Janet stood in the doorway of the room and looked around, then she turned to him again, a sparkle in her eyes that created that dichotomy in him again. "And if I *don't* want my own room?"

"Then I'm in here." He carried the bags into his bedroom, which had once been an upstairs parlor. He'd moved the old furniture into the attic and moved in a California queen-size sleigh bed. The room accommodated a large desk, a full-size dresser in a plain, functional style and an overstuffed chair he'd brought up from downstairs to put near the fireplace.

"Wow." Janet went to the fireplace and touched the columns and capitals that flanked the elegant piece created from three different kinds of marble. "Isn't this something special?" she asked.

"I'm not sure," he admitted, putting the bags down near the closet. "But I remember my grandmother sitting there with her knitting when this was a parlor."

She walked across the room to look out the window. "No wonder the room's so huge. What would I see out there if it was still light?"

"Lilacs, when they're in bloom, and roses from our neighbor across the backyard. Beyond their house is a view of the ocean."

She turned and went to the bed, tested it with her hands, then sat on it. "Ah," she said. "You're a lover of hard mattresses."

He guessed she didn't approve. That saddened him. He hated the thought of her sleeping across the hall.

"Does that mean you want your bags in Grandma's room?"

She swung her legs up onto the bed, then boosted herself until she was near the pillows. "No, it doesn't." She patted the place beside her. "I'd sleep on concrete to be near you. But my preference is a little softer than this."

Relieved, he went to sit beside her on the thick, dark-blue coverlet. He put an arm around her and she leaned into him.

"But this is such a haven. Would *you* prefer to sleep alone?" She tipped her head back to look at him. "You can be honest. You could still invite me across the hall at any time. You're probably very used to having your privacy and space."

"I am very used to that." He held her closer. She swung a leg over his. "And I'd like to remember that as the way things *used* to be."

"Can I put my things in your closet?"

"Yes."

"And my makeup on the bathroom counter?"

"Yes."

"Can I have a drawer for my underwear?"

"Sure."

She wrapped an arm around his waist. "You've just passed the cohabitation test."

"As soon as we finish your investigation," he said, "we should pool our skills. Why don't you take over the space I was going to use for a coffee shop. Then you won't have to worry about a good location. We can work together, be together."

She sat up on her knees and wrapped her arms around him. Had he been smaller, she might have cut off his air.

"That's genius!" she said. "I would love that!"

"We'll research fixtures and supplies as soon as we find out what was going on with your aunt."

She sighed, their little bubble burst by that small reminder of reality. Wouldn't it be wonderful, he thought, if they were just two people unencumbered by their convoluted pasts?

But they weren't.

"I'm going to call Dean Ballard," he said, "and see if he can help us find your aunt's boyfriend. Would you make some coffee while I do that? We'll add Irish Cream to it."

She swung her legs off the bed. "Already enslaved in the kitchen," she joked. "Okay. Regular or decaf?"

"Whatever you want."

"Strong?"

"Please."

JANET FOUND a Mr. Coffee on an old wooden block counter in the kitchen. The room was mostly yellow, with floor-to-counter cupboards. There was a yellow stove and refrigerator, and a bookcase that held cookbooks on the bottom shelves, but all kinds of small appliances and bric-a-brac on the top three.

A long, farm-style table with a plank top occupied a window corner of the room, with four solid chairs. She loved this place.

After finding the coffee, Janet filled the basket, then the water well and plugged the pot in. She half expected sparks to fly out at her, but the little red light went on without incident. Coffee began to drip into the carafe in no time.

"Dean's on the case," Brian announced, walking into the room. He went to the refrigerator for a bottle of Irish Cream, then pulled two mugs down from an upper cupboard.

He left the things on the counter and came to sit at a right angle to her. "So, you just have to find something to keep you busy in the house for a couple of days. He's confident it won't take long, but you never know."

"If I can use the computer I saw on your desk," she suggested, "I can look up some of your antiques, and try to get an idea for you of what to keep, what to give away. And I can check out sources for equipment for the coffee shop."

"Good. I've got to catch up the books for the shop, and I've got all that on my laptop."

When the coffee was finished, he poured it into their cups and added Irish Cream, then they sat in the dark on an old gold velvet settee and made plans for their future.

Later that night, Janet awoke, spooned into his body, his strong arm wrapped around her. She felt safe and happy, and wondered for the first time since the wedding how China was doing.

She was certain her sister was secure and happy in Campbell's love, but realizing that she hadn't thought about her in several days shocked her. They'd been each other's first thought for so long—until the boxes hidden in their parents' attic had sent them on separate searches. And even then they'd kept in touch, promising each other that whatever they discovered they would always be sisters.

Now they were both part of the wonderful Abbott family—Janet by birth and China by marriage. Janet wanted so much to relieve her brothers' minds about the kidnapping. She paused to say a silent prayer that Brian's friend Dean would find her aunt Kate's boyfriend and, hopefully, the reason Abby was taken.

Janet appreciated all Brian had done to help her and was cautiously hopeful that his suggestion that they "work together, be together" was just the first step toward the future she envisioned.

She prayed also that Brian would always know how

much she loved him, and that together they could create the family he'd never had.

That done, she leaned into him and went back to sleep.

"I'VE G-T SOME—NG." Dean Ballard's voice came muffled and broken up over Brian's cell phone. Janet was researching in his office, and he sat at the kitchen table, book work spread around him.

"Uh, say that again, Dean." Brian thought he'd interpreted the message, but only a day had passed. "You've got something?"

"Yeah. I'm coming over."

"Okay. I'm at home."

"What? Why aren't you working?"

"Long story. I'll explain when you get here."

"Okay. Is there beer in this for me?"

"Sure."

Brian went upstairs to tell Janet. She sat in his desk chair, staring at an image on the computer screen of a Tiffany lamp just like the one in the living room. She'd spent all the previous day finding values and markets for many of the items downstairs he thought he'd be willing to part with.

"Hey," he called from the doorway. "Miss Antiques Road Show."

"Brian!" she said.

She turned to him, a broad grin on her face. He loved the way she always did that. After his father's dark looks at him, and his mother's sadness, Janet's joy at the sight of him gave him an indescribable high.

"Do you know what that lamp is worth? Would you believe ten thousand dollars?"

"Cool. Dean just called."

She dropped her feet. The joy gone, her expression was now anxious. "And?"

"He's got something. He's coming over."

She ran across the room to him and wrapped her arms around him. "Thank goodness! Did he give you any details?"

"No. Only that he's coming over and he wants beer."

"Where was he? When will he be here?"

She'd just posed the question when a rap sounded on the downstairs door. "Now," he said.

She ran down the stairs ahead of him.

Dean Ballard lived on a mahogany-trimmed, thirties-era houseboat that always reminded Brian of the *Busted Flush,* the boat Travis McGee owned in the John D. MacDonald detective novels. Except that instead of winning it in a poker game, Dean had inherited it from a girlfriend who'd died at twenty-eight of inoperable cancer.

Dean had the sensitive but cynical playboy style of McGee, though his detective work was more along the lines of divorce surveillance, finding missing teenagers, adoption searches. He often complained that his self-defense classes had been a waste.

He was tall and fit and bemoaned his bright red hair and the freckles that went with it.

Brian introduced him to Janet. Dean shook her hand. "I've read about you in the paper," he said. "After all that's happened in this world, having you restored to

your family has been like a breath of hope to everyone."
He frowned. "How's it been for you?"

Brian headed for the kitchen and glanced over his
shoulder, to see Janet smile confidingly as they followed. "It's been pretty wonderful," she replied. "But
there's still mystery surrounding why I was taken. And
I'd like to solve that for my family. Did Brian explain
to you that the Abbotts' nanny and my adoptive mother's sister are one and the same person?"

"Yes, he did." They'd reached the table and Dean
dropped a folder on it. "And I think I've got your aunt's
boyfriend for you."

She sank onto a chair at the table while Brian got
Dean's beer and poured coffee for himself and Janet.
Once they were all seated, Dean opened the folder, then
looked up at them with a grin.

"To be honest," he said, "this was so easy I almost
don't deserve the beer. Kate Bellows's boyfriend is mentioned in the police report of all the original interviews
at the time of the kidnapping and is identified as a friend
of your aunt's. His name was Zachary Bristol. He and
his brother, Peter, worked for—" he turned to Brian
"—your father, Corbin Girard."

Brian frowned, a vague memory coming back to him
of two brothers employed in the gardens. His mother
hadn't liked them because one of them had overpruned
the hydrangea, and when she'd complained he'd re-
sponded rudely. She'd told Brian's father—something
she seldom did regarding the staff; she usually took
care of problems herself.

"Story goes that he once showed up drunk at Shepherd's Knoll to see Kate." Dean relayed the contents of the report. "Apparently, Mrs. Abbott sent him away. Obviously, he was suspected of a revenge motive in the kidnapping, but he had a tight alibi for that night. Several witnesses said he was in the corner booth of his favorite watering hole. The owner claimed he always closed the place and Zachary was there till last call."

Janet was wide-eyed. "Is he…still alive?" she asked.

Dean nodded. "I tracked him to a men's mission in Yonkers. He's close to seventy. No serious criminal record, but drunk most of his life. His brother died four years ago." Dean handed Brian his business card. "Address of the mission on the back. Visitors welcome anytime. It's about an hour and a half drive."

"We have to go there," Janet said to Brian.

"Why don't I go," Brian suggested, "and locate him for you. A men's mission isn't the best place…"

"I'll get my purse," she said, no longer listening to him.

Dean took a pull on his beer. "She's going with you," he said.

"Yeah." Brian ran a hand over his face. "That's a very determined woman."

Dean seemed to agree. "You should be able to understand that, being a stubborn cuss yourself."

"Thanks, buddy," Brian said, pretending injury. "I was looking for sympathy and support."

Dean's eyes widened. "From me?"

"Really. What was I thinking?"

Dean pushed his chair back, stood and patted Brian's shoulder. "Well, call me if I can do anything else."

Brian got to his feet to shake his hand. "Thanks, Dean. I appreciate your help."

"Happy to oblige. Let me know how it turns out—if that's not too personal."

"Sure."

Janet was back, with her purse slung over her shoulder and a determined look on her face. "Ready?" she asked Brian.

He wasn't sure he was, but he led the way out anyway.

Chapter Twelve

The Night Light Men's Mission was housed in a converted mill on the Hudson River. The building was brick and dreary, but the bright neon sign with the name of the mission promised "food and the Word."

Brian looked out at the men sitting on the sidewalk in front.

"I know you're wishing I'd stayed home," she said, unlocking her door. "But I'm here, and the sooner I find out what happened, the better everything will be."

"Okay. Just stay with me."

"No problem there."

Brian circled his truck to walk her into the building. "If my vehicle's in pieces when we come out," he warned, clearly attempting to lighten the mood, "you owe me."

She squeezed the hand she held. "I owe you for a lot more than that."

An older man answered the bell. He was short and slight, longish gray hair slicked back in an attempt at good grooming. He looked at them briefly, his bright blue watery eyes expressing surprise, then let them in.

"Hello," Janet said. "I'd like to see Zachary Bristol, if that's possible."

He didn't seem sure that it was, but he led them to an office, where a sturdy man in a blue polo shirt reviewed paperwork on an old teacher's desk.

"Father Mark," the old man said. "These people would like to see Bristol."

Father Mark looked up, then stood and came around the desk to introduce himself, as the little man disappeared. He was very tall and balding and had a calmness about him Janet wanted to absorb if she'd had the time. And it would take time to get her from nervous wreck to serene woman.

He sat them in a pair of chairs that faced his desk, then returned to his chair.

"Will you tell me what you want with him?" the priest asked.

Janet explained with only necessary detail how she'd been kidnapped and that the whole thing remained a mystery to this day. She told him about the Abbotts' nanny and her adoptive mother's sister being the same woman. "We think she took me," Janet said, "but that she was possibly an accomplice to the man she was in love with."

The priest nodded. "Zachary Bristol."

"Yes." Janet sat on the edge of her chair and leaned toward the desk, her need to know so desperate she wasn't sure how she prevented herself from running through the building, screaming Bristol's name until she found him. Unless it was the sad, wise look in the priest's eyes.

"My family's suffered so much," she said. "You can imagine my mother's agony. My father died without knowing whether I was dead or alive, and each of my older brothers assumed blame for the fact that I was taken. That's a sort of self-inflicted child's guilt, but sometimes that's the hardest to recover from. Please, Father. I have to see him."

The priest nodded. "Of course you do. I can't stop you, but I have to explain that he's old and frail and dying of liver disease. The doctor says he has a month, probably less. Prosecution wouldn't—"

Janet interrupted him with a shake of her head. "That's not my purpose. I just have to find out what happened so that my family can be at peace."

"All right." He pushed his chair back from the desk, but hesitated before getting to his feet. "You have to be prepared for the fact that he's a hard case," he said. "He's been drunk most of his life, and the only friend he had in the world was his brother, who died several years ago. I don't think he regrets anything."

Janet nodded. "I'm not looking for some reformed good-at-heart bad guy who regrets what he did to us and wants to make amends before he dies. I just want to know what happened."

"Okay. Follow me. He's in the backyard."

A beautiful lawn ran for a considerable distance, then sloped down to the river. Several picnic tables were set up there and a frail old man sat at one, smoking a cigarette.

A loud buzzer rang from inside the building, and the

priest stopped in his tracks. "That's Zack at the table. Excuse me, please. I'll have to let you introduce yourselves."

Janet felt her insides churning as she approached the table and sat down opposite Zachary Bristol. Brian sat beside her.

The man assessed her suspiciously, eyes narrowed through the smoke from his cigarette. "Yeah?" The question was hostile.

Hate and anger obviously remained in a body emaciated from illness and a lifetime of alcohol consumption. Sallow skin was pulled tightly over the angular bones of his face. His eyes were dark, his hands bony as he lifted the half-smoked cigarette to a tight, trembling mouth.

"What?" he demanded. He studied Brian. "You cops? I didn't have nothing to do with the missing donation money."

Janet looked into strangely bright eyes and didn't know what to say. That he'd repelled contact all his life was easy to see. She found herself wondering what had happened to him to cause that, then how she could reach him to make him tell her what had happened.

"We don't care about that," Brian said. "We want to ask you a few questions about a lady in your past."

He cocked a gnarly eyebrow, looking interested. "Yeah? Who?"

"Kate Bellows."

Bristol made a scornful sound and took another puff of his cigarette. "Big girl," he said. "A real leaner. But hot stuff."

"What do you mean by a leaner?" Janet asked.

He shrugged. The action made him cough. "She was lookin' for a man to lean on," he said. "Wasn't very pretty. Like I said, big girl. Good in bed, though." He seemed pleased about that. "So was I in those days. Maybe too good, I guess. She wanted me bad. Said she'd spent most of her life avoiding men like me, but finally decided life was too short."

Janet remembered her "funny" Aunt Kate and tried to imagine Bristol in his younger days, hoping to find some clue to what it was about him that would have appealed to her. Unless it was that loneliness had finally made Kate desperate.

Then something seemed to occur to Bristol, and he straightened abruptly. His eyes flared. "Are you her kid? Did she send you to pass yourself off as mine to try to get my Social Security? 'Cause I never had a kid. Ever."

"No." Janet spoke in a calm voice but asked directly, "I came here to find out if you helped Kate steal the Abbott baby."

His eyes widened, then narrowed to slits, his whole being expanding, then contracting with a labored breath. He put the cigarette to his lips again. "I didn't steal the Abbott baby," he said.

It was a lie. Janet was sure of it but didn't know how to prove it.

"We know you did," Brian said in an even voice, his gaze holding Bristol's. "All the new testing picked up your DNA off the doll she had with her."

Janet barely prevented herself from turning to Brian

in openmouthed surprise. That was a bald-faced lie, but Bristol listened.

"Your days are numbered, Bristol," Brian went on, "and the family's got her back now. So, you're not going to jail. Everybody involved would just like to know why you did it."

Bristol stared at Janet, more curiosity that regret in his eyes. "That you?" he asked.

"Yes," she replied. "Please tell me why."

He butted his cigarette on the tabletop and folded his skeletal arms on it. "She was always talking about having babies, but knew she shouldn't have any cause she liked to move around. So she just took care of other people's, instead. But she felt bad for her sister in California, who wanted kids and couldn't have them. Talked about her all the time.

"Anyway, I was working on the property next door and she and I met a couple of times at that bar…Combustible. You know…the bar? She was hot for me and I liked her well enough. We used to meet sometimes in the thick trees between the properties. We were a couple of middle-aged sexpots, and we had a good time together."

Janet tried to think of her vague aunt Kate as hot for any man and simply couldn't. What she'd done had apparently changed her in every way.

Bristol had a coughing fit and shook out another cigarette. "I went to visit her," he said when the coughing quieted. He hit the end of a lighter and held the cigarette to the flame. "But that high-and-mighty Mrs. Abbott threw me out. Girard had just fired me 'cause his lady complained about the way I trimmed the hydrangea."

He drew on the cigarette, closed his eyes so that he wouldn't be distracted, then blew out, solemnly attentive to the ritual.

"I was tired," he continued finally, "of the people in the big houses pushing me around. Mrs. Abbott had this beautiful baby in her arms, and I got this idea." He paused for effect. Janet felt a chill ripple through her at the easy way he said that.

"Kate didn't want to do it at first, till I told her we'd send the baby to her sister. Then her eyes lit up. It was so simple. She got the baby out of her bed and carried her to the basement window, where I was waiting so nobody'd hear the front door. She said those boys never missed anything. She gave me the money for Pete's girlfriend—Pete's my brother," he added in an aside, "so that she could take the baby to Kate's sister and tell her it was ours and that she couldn't raise her anymore.

"Pete's girl—I don't even remember her name now—said Kate's sister was very happy to have the baby. She said her face just lit up." He sighed and had another coughing fit. There was death in the sound. "Your aunt wanted us to get married later," he continued, "but I didn't like the idea of her telling me what to do any more than I liked those rich biddies telling me. And she got downright loopy after a while. Finally went home to be near her sister."

"Did you pay the owner of the bar," Brian asked, "to tell the police you'd been there drinking all night?"

He shook his head. "My brother wore my jacket and my hat and sat in my booth all night so I'd have an alibi."

"And no one knew what you'd done." Janet heard her own voice filled with the cumulative pain of all the Abbotts, and the father who'd died unaware that she was safe.

"Well…" He sighed, a furrow of confusion on his brow. "One person did."

Janet sat up and felt Brian react beside her. "Who?" she gasped.

"My boss knew."

"You mean…Corbin Girard? Why?"

"Because I ran with the baby through the trees that separate the properties to get to the car I'd left on the road. The old man was coming home and turned into his driveway as I was coming out of the trees. His headlights picked me out, but I got into my car and took off before he could stop. I was sure I was had. I kept reading the papers about the kidnapping, thinking they'd quote him as sayin' he saw somebody runnin' away with the baby, but he didn't." Bristol shook his head. "That was one hateful old bastard to everyone around him—his wife, his kid, everybody. And I guess he even hated the neighbors, 'cause he didn't tell the police what he saw."

JANET WEPT in Brian's arms all evening. They sat on the sofa while he encouraged her to drink a little brandy and she purged herself of the grief she'd taken on for the entire family.

"What a tragic old man," she said over and over. "How do you get to a place where you blame everyone else for your shortcomings and exact revenge for a slight by ripping a family apart?"

For a moment, he wasn't sure if she'd defined Bristol's character or his own father's. But he'd realized as he listened to her talk that she hadn't considered Corbin Girard's part, except to ask Brian why he was surprised that his father hadn't said anything.

"He's been cruel and hateful to his wife and to you," she said. "He tried to burn down Shepherd's Knoll. Why would he care that I'd been stolen? Why wouldn't you assume he'd just enjoy it because it hurt my family?"

What Brian didn't understand was why she continued to hold on to *him* while she said that. He did his best to comfort her, but had been in a shocked state of disbelief since Bristol had said those fateful words: "My boss knew."

His father had let the family suffer for an entire generation, let Nathan Abbott die without knowing that his daughter was safe. Even Brian, who'd suffered his father's hatred all his life, couldn't comprehend the depth of that cruelty.

And knowing that, he saw the future he and Janet had planned erase itself completely. Knowing that his past would rear its ugly head repeatedly to embarrass her and the family had been one thing; knowing that he was made of the man who'd stood silently by while Janet was lost to her family for twenty-five years was something else entirely.

He couldn't spend his life with her under those circumstances.

"The best thing you could do," he said, "now that you know everything, is go home and explain it to your family. Deal with it together. Get it out of the way. Then the Abbotts will finally be whole again."

"I want to," she said, still holding on to him. "But I want to stay with you one more night. I need to just… lose it all in you. Is that okay?"

"Of course." He wasn't sure he could come out of one more night with his heart whole, but this had never been about *his* heart, anyway.

They showered together, then made love in the middle of his bed until the moon was high. They slept entangled for several hours, then he awoke to her lips on his, and they made love again with a feverish desperation that made sense to both of them—she, because her love for Brian grounded her and helped her see through the sadness and pain she had to explain to her family and would help her carry them to the other side; he, because he knew this was goodbye.

A Realtor from Montauk had already spoken to him once about a retired restaurateur who wanted to buy the store. All he had to do was call her, name a price, and he could be gone before the week was out.

He hadn't counted, though, on Janet's ability to read his thoughts. She'd showered first after breakfast. When he came out of the shower, she was brushing her hair— an action that always put him a little off his game. He guessed it was the way the redwood highlights rippled, making her look a little as though she wore a halo. Now that he'd made love to her, he knew her hair's silken touch along his body.

"I'll be back tomorrow morning?" she asked, putting the brush down and fluffing her hair with her fingers. "I should e-mail the shop in Boston that offered to buy the Matt Morgan vase."

"Don't you want to be with your family for a few days?" he asked, looking into the same mirror over the dresser that she used, while being careful not to meet her eyes. He combed a hand through hair that was already smooth. "Besides, I won't be here. I'm going to the shop. I've got a lot of catching up to do." That sounded insensitive and lame, but he pretended not to notice.

"Do you want me to bring some of this home? I can work on my laptop."

"Don't worry about it," he said, turning away from the mirror and going to the bedside table for his wallet and keys. "There's plenty of time…"

When he turned around again, she was standing in front of him, arms folded, mouth in a firm line.

"I felt this coming on this morning," she said, a lingering sadness in her eyes. He wasn't sure if that sadness was left over from yesterday, or created by this moment. "When you were making love to me there was something…final about it."

He'd have preferred time to think about how to tell her this, but she was always a step ahead of him.

He caught her arm and pulled her down beside him

on the edge of the bed. "Let me explain this to you," he said, "without interruption, okay?"

She yanked her arm away. "You'll be sure and let me know when I get to talk."

"Janet…"

"Go on. Explain yourself."

He was usually good at organizing his thoughts. But sorrow was difficult to put into order.

"I love you more than anything," he said quickly. He was certain of that. "And I'd rather die than contribute more pain to what's already been really difficult for you."

She opened her mouth to comment, but he raised an index finger to remind her of her agreement. She swept a hand between them, inviting him to go on.

"But consider what's happened," he implored. "I was sure that my past was going to rear up and pounce on us every time something good happened to the Abbotts or they ended up in the paper."

The argument was in her eyes, but she bit her lip and remained quiet.

"Okay, maybe I'm more sensitive to that than you are, but I worried about it. Only, spending time with you, falling in love with you, made me believe that we could deal with it, that all that matters is what we feel for each other."

She nodded in agreement, then she looked wary as she waited for the other shoe to drop.

He made himself speak firmly, as though the matter was settled and precluded discussion. "But there's no way we can live around the fact that my father knew who abducted you and never said a word. My father let your parents and your brothers live without you for twenty-five years. Not only live without you but unaware if you were dead or alive."

"Is it my turn yet?" she asked.

"No," he replied. "Try to hear what I'm saying. It may not matter to you because you lived it in a completely different way than your family did. You were loved and happy and probably even spoiled. The Abbotts were in agony in the beginning, then in a sort of half-life later where they forced themselves to function. They have you back, but that was twenty-five years of their lives. The whole formative period of your brothers' lives. There's no way I can push myself between you and them and ask that they let me have you so that I can be happy."

She got to her feet and put a hand firmly over his mouth. It smelled of soap and toothpaste. "I'm taking my turn to speak."

He pulled her hand down. "I'm not finished."

"Oh, yes, you are!" she snapped. "In the first place, the man who kept quiet and let all this go on was your father, not you. In the second place, my family welcomed you into their lives, and I'm sure would be hurt abominably to know that you think so little of their humanity. And in the *third* place, it is not their job to *let you have me,* as you put it. Who I choose to spend my life with is *my* decision. Brian. Please. Don't do this to us."

"Before you knew me I was not an admirable person," he said mercilessly. "Remember what I told you about Cordie?" Janet opened her mouth, probably to insist that he'd changed, but he talked over her. "Right. I'm not that man anymore, but when your family knows what my father did, that he saw someone running away with you and never told, they'll remember the old me. Maybe not now, but there'll be resentment and anger from somebody, and rightly so. How can I put you in a position where you'd have to choose between your husband and your brothers?"

"They'd never blame you," she told him tearfully.

"It'll always be there, waiting to rear its ugly head. And if your brothers don't bring it up, the press will."

She folded her arms stubbornly. "How are they going to find out? They haven't in all this time."

"They find out everything." That was grim certainty.

She stared at him, speechless. He saw in her tortured eyes that she accepted her argument was lost.

"I'm leaving in a matter of days," he said, determined to crush whatever hope she might be trying to maintain. "A Realtor has had a buyer for the store for months. It'd be wisest to go back home and forget all the things we've talked about."

"How would you know?" she asked, snatching up her purse. "You wouldn't recognize wisdom if it fell on your head. Are you taking me home?"

"Yes." He followed her into the hallway, thinking the altercation was over and a little surprised that he'd survived, when she spun on him and wanged him with her purse.

Apparently, it wasn't over after all.

"You know what just frosts me to the bone?" she demanded.

He kept an eye on her purse. "What?"

"That I love you so much!" she said, her voice falling from a shout to a throaty whisper as tears overtook her. "That I believed you when you made love to me. That I thought I'd found my place in a wonderful family, and that I was going to start another one with you."

Had she dug his heart out with a trowel, she could not have hurt him more.

She spun around again, purse flying, and ran along the hallway and down the stairs.

Chapter Thirteen

Killian and Chloe were home when Janet stormed into the house, almost colliding with Winfield in her haste to put as much distance between herself and Brian as possible.

"Nice to have you back, Janet," Winfield said, picking up the mail that had blown off the credenza as she'd flown past.

"Thank you, Winfield." She held tightly to her purse strap, afraid she would scream at any moment. "Where is everyone?"

"The honeymooners are still away," he replied. "Daniel has taken Cordie to town, Kezia is in the kitchen with the children, Tante Bijou is napping and your mother and brother are in the library. Is something wrong?"

"I'm fine," she lied. "Thank you, Winfield." She hurried toward the library, still clutching the strap of her purse. She knocked on the door and without waiting for anyone to answer, pushed her way in.

Her mother and Killian sat on the leather sofa. Chloe rose at the sight of her, her expression concerned. She put a hand to her heart. "What? What's happened? Is it Sawyer? Campbell?"

"No, no." Janet stopped several feet from them, her composure collapsing and with it her entire world. "Everyone's okay." She began to weep. "Nothing's wrong. Just…just me!"

Chloe opened her arms and Janet ran into them.

"Oh, now." Chloe patted her back and rocked her as though she were two years old. "Certainly all this anguish isn't over the sale of a property."

"No. I lied to you," she admitted, now sobbing. "I didn't go to L.A. to sell a property."

Chloe urged her down onto the sofa and sat beside her, an arm still around her. "Now, what can be this bad?"

Janet closed her eyes. If she only knew. There was so much to tell, so much she didn't want to remember.

Killian knelt beside her and handed her a cup of coffee. "Drink this," he said. "It's good strong stuff."

"I have to tell you…"

"Have some coffee first."

She complied, and felt the hot brew stream into her stomach.

"A little more. Your knees look ready to buckle."

She took the second sip and a moment later felt ever so slightly more alive, but as miserable as she felt, that wasn't necessarily better. She drew a deep breath, and suddenly, a weird calm settled over her body. It occurred to her that this was odd. Caffeine was supposed to stimulate your nerves. Maybe this twilight zone she was in applied to everything, even coffee.

Killian pulled up a chair facing her and her mother. "If you didn't go home to sell property, why did you go?" he asked.

Slowly, stopping to sob occasionally, she told them the whole story, from her discovery of the photograph in the album, which matched her picture of her aunt, to Brian's suspicion that the boyfriend Janet's mother claimed had changed her aunt had to be from Kate's days in Losthampton.

As they stared at her in disbelief, she told them about spending three days at Brian's, about his friend Dean's investigation, about talking to Zachary Bristol. Then she told them what he'd said about Corbin Girard.

Chloe gasped and Killian stood and paced across the room. He said words that made Chloe gasp again. Then she said a few things in French, which Janet suspected were no less profane.

Killian walked to the back of the sofa and wrapped his arms around both of them. "I'm going to talk to the district attorney, so that if Girard ever does get out of the hospital, we'll have something else to charge him with. I'd like to see that bag of hate go away for a long time." He squeezed her shoulder. "But we're not going to dwell on it. It's good to have the answers, Janet. So now that we know what happened and we have you back, our family life starts all over."

Janet burst into sobs again.

"*Chère,* what is it?" Chloe asked, holding her close. "Please. You're not happy here?"

"Oh, *maman*." That was so far from the truth that Janet wasn't certain how to deny it. "It isn't about us."

"Then what is it about?"

"Ah." Killian's hand ruffled her hair. "It's love, isn't it? It's Brian."

Janet looked up at him in astonishment. "How do you always know what's going on, when you're never around?"

"My family," he said simply, "my job. What happened? You need me to go beat him up for you?"

"Please," she said, heaving a sigh. "Twice would be nice."

"Well, tell me about it. Then we'll decide if twice is necessary. Or if I'll just do a really good job the first time."

"OH, HELL!" Brian said under his voice. He'd just walked into Hudson River Ice Cream for an iced mocha and a pint of barber pole to cool his frantic brain, when he spotted Cordie Abbott standing at the counter. She was hard to miss these days, her pregnancy with twins jutting out before her like a boat under full sail.

He made an effort to dredge up a smile, but wasn't sure if his mouth complied. His entire being was in the claw of a dark depression. He felt sure he'd done the right thing with Janet—for her sake and for the Abbotts'—but living with the decision would be another matter.

He'd called the Realtor from his cell phone the moment he'd dropped Janet off, then he'd stopped to pick up an outboard they'd been repairing for him at the automotive shop. He'd wanted a mocha for the drive home, and a little barber-pole ice cream to get him through the packing.

Cordie smiled at him as he went to stand beside her, but she seemed less animated than usual, the corners of her mouth a little tight. She'd apparently been shopping. A small paper bag with handles dangled from her fingers.

"Hi," he said. "Have you come for your barber-pole ice-cream fix?"

"Yeah. I've been trying to walk off a backache."

"Are you here by yourself?"

"No, I left Daniel at the market to pick up some things for Kezia, and told him I'd take a short walk and meet him back there." She looped an arm in his and leaned a little. "Are you okay?" she asked. "You look grim. Did you and Janet just get home?"

He wasn't sure how to answer that. "I just dropped her off at the house," he said. That was true enough.

"Did something go wrong with the sale of her property?"

"I'm sure she'll tell you all about it." Evading a lie was getting tricky.

She frowned at him as though she wanted to question him further, then she rolled her eyes in disgust and handed him a five-dollar bill and the bag she held. "Brian, I'm sorry. Would you pay for my order while I run into the ladies' room. I swear, I can't get more than ten feet from one lately."

"Sure. I'll be happy to."

He'd paid for her order, gotten his own and was about to ask one of the girls behind the counter to check on Cordie, when she waddled out of the bathroom, close to tears.

"What?" he asked, taking her arm.

She pushed him through the doorway into the sunlight. "Brian. Can you handle some frank pregnant woman talk?"

He couldn't, but she appeared frightened and a little desperate.

"Shoot."

"My water broke while I was in the bathroom," she blurted.

"Oh, God. Okay. Not a problem." He started to lead her toward the rental car, which he still hadn't returned. And thank goodness for that. He wouldn't have wanted to get her up into the cab of his truck. "I'll drive you, but I've seen enough hospital movies to know that you still have a little time…"

"Maybe a *little* problem," she said, clearly about to lose her battle with the tears. "Are you still okay with this? You're not going to collapse in a puddle of testosterone?"

He opened the back door. "Of course not. The hospital's only a few miles away. But…what little problem?"

She gulped a sob. "Brian…I felt *fingers!*"

"Fingers," he repeated, failing to understand her. "What do you…" Then it dawned on him. "A *baby's* fingers?"

"Yeah."

She sat on the edge of the back seat and levered herself backward.

"Isn't the head supposed to come first?"

"Yes! That means the baby isn't positioned correctly!"

Oh, *God!* "Okay, don't panic." He dug out his cell phone as she backed all the way onto the seat. He dialed 911, tossed their bags onto the floor in the back and closed the door.

"Nine-one-one. What is your emergency?" a calm voice asked as he tore open his door.

"I'm heading for the hospital with a woman pregnant with twins," he said, throwing himself behind the wheel. "Her water broke, and she said she feels fingers!"

"What's her due date?" the operator asked.

Who the hell cared? he thought in terror. Didn't the operator hear him? Cordie felt *fingers!*

Brian shouted the question at Cordie as he closed his door, then turned on the ignition.

"October seventeenth," she shouted back. "What should I do?"

"I heard her," said the voice on the other end of the line. "Tell her to bend her legs and keep her bottom up as much as possible so gravity doesn't work against us. Hold on. I'm going to get the E.R. on the line."

Brian took advantage of the brief lull in conversation to check the traffic, then pull out onto the highway in the direction of the hospital.

"The doctor wants to know if this is her first," the operator said.

Brian thought so. "First baby, Cordie?"

"Yes!"

"What did the fluid look like?"

Brian repeated the question to Cordie.

"Oh…ah…clear, mostly, with little flecks of white stuff."

Brian saw a green light turn yellow up ahead and tried to run it, but had to brake at the last moment. "Hold on, Cordie!" he cautioned.

He felt her hand slap the top of the back seat.

He repeated her answer to the operator, he himself experiencing definite symptoms of some cardiac event. Or maybe it was just a panic attack.

"The doctor says that's good, but tell her not to push," the operator stated. "To keep calm and just breathe through the contractions. How far away are you?"

"About a mile," Brian said, "but I'm stuck at a red light."

"A police unit will come up behind you any minute now to escort you the rest of the way. Both of you just relax. You're close enough to make it in time."

"Okay. Cordie, the doctor says not to push!" He had to shout the order because Cordie was growling in distress.

"I know! I'm not pushing, but one baby's pushing me!"

"Cordie," he pleaded, "please don't let him—or her!—out until we get to the hospital, because I am not pulling over! Ah…here's our escort! Hold on. Police car's going to get us through the traffic!"

There was another protracted growl, then a deep sigh. "Did you get my bag?"

He couldn't quite believe the question. He checked the rearview mirror and saw only her hand gripping the back of the seat.

"What bag?" he asked.

"The one I gave you to hold. It's for Killian!"

"Cordie, what does it matter at this…?"

"It's something else to think about!" she shouted at him. "And it's for Killian! Did you get it?"

"Yes!" he shouted back. "It's on the floor back there. Forget it, please, and focus on keeping the babies inside until we get to the hospital! I'll take care of the bag when we get there."

The police unit arrived, and the officer waved at him as he passed, turned on his lights and siren and led him away just as the light changed.

Cordie was in the middle of another, more desperate growl as Brian followed the officer into the hospital's parking lot and to the Emergency entrance.

A doctor and a nurse ran out with a gurney, and Brian and the officer helped them lift Cordie onto it. She grabbed Brian's hand. "Please phone Killian," she said, "and find Daniel. He'll be frantic. Daniel's cell is—"

She shouted the number at him as the doctor and nurse began to push the gurney inside.

"Okay, don't worry!" he called after her. Brian pulled out his cell phone and began to follow, but the police officer stopped him. He was tall and young and smiling. "You have to make your calls out here. Can't use a cell phone in there."

"Right." He should have thought of that. "Thanks for running interference for us."

"Sure. Babies are always worth the hurry. I'll follow her in."

He phoned Daniel first, afraid he'd forget the number. The man sounded desperate. "Thank God!" he said. "I couldn't imagine what happened to her, but I didn't know how I was going to tell Killian that I'd lost his wife and babies."

"I'll call him right now. You'd better go pick him up."

"Right. Thanks, Brian."

Winfield answered the phone, then Killian came on the line.

"Hi!" Brian said, determined not to mention the harried trip to the hospital or the scary fingers. He was sure Killian would find out everything when he got there. "It's Brian. You're having the babies, Killian. Daniel's on his way to pick you up."

"What? Oh, my God!" Killian sounded frantic. "But how did you...?"

"I'll explain when you get here. Don't leave without Daniel."

"But he was driving her..."

"I know. But she's fine, and I'll tell you all about it when you get here."

Remembering he'd promised Cordie he'd take care of the bag for Killian, Brian reached into the car for it before walking into the E.R.

Brian met the police officer just inside the waiting room. "Mr. Girard. Come on, I'll show you where to wait for news of your sister-in-law. You need coffee, or something?"

Brian grinned, just beginning to relax a little. Poor Cordie and her babies probably weren't out of the woods, but at least her safety was now in competent hands.

"She's not my sister-in-law."

The officer looked confused. "I'm sorry. She told me to tell her brother-in-law what was happening. That isn't you?"

"Ah…" It was harder to deny if she'd said it. "Well, it's…complicated."

"Okay. My life gets complicated, too."

"Thanks again for your help."

"That's my job." He led Brian down a long hallway and into a small waiting area with blue upholstered sofa and chairs, a television mounted on the wall and a table covered with magazines.

With a parting wave, the officer left him.

A nurse appeared almost immediately. She looked like a veteran and wore a tired but cheerful smile. "You Mrs. Abbott's brother-in-law?" she asked.

To just say yes was easier.

"Mrs. Abbott wanted to make sure you called her husband."

"I did," he confirmed.

"And that you have her bag."

He held it up. Unfortunately, when he'd grabbed it out of the car he'd caught the bag on its side, and when he lifted it to show the nurse, a clump of blue lace fell onto his hand. He caught it before it hit the floor. Panties. He quickly returned them to the bag and saw the matching bra. Cordie, he guessed, was planning ahead. For Killian.

That made him smile for the first time since he'd run into her earlier. The nurse smiled, too. "No wonder she didn't want to part with those. I'll be back as soon as I can with a report."

"Thank you." He put Cordie's things in the chair beside him. He imagined the ice cream was still in its bag, melting into a puddle in the back seat of his rental car.

This had been a very challenging day.

And a strange one for a man who'd always tried hard to belong but felt as though he never had.

He hadn't belonged in his own family, and he'd thought he couldn't really belong to the Abbotts because Susannah, his mother, never really had. She'd borne two sons for Nathan, but she'd never understood the heart and spirit of the family.

He did belong to Janet, heart and soul. But he couldn't belong to her in actuality because of everything his family had done to hers.

Still, her image lived behind his eyes, and though it had been only hours since he'd last seen her, it felt like forever.

And here he was in this alien environment in charge of a woman's purse and blue lace underwear.

God.

He picked up a *Sports Illustrated* off the table and tried to get involved in a story about blue-water fishing.

Killian arrived five minutes later as though he'd been launched. Trailing in his wake were Chloe and Daniel, but there was no sign of Janet. Brian wondered if she hadn't come because she'd known he'd be here.

No. She would be here in support of her brother, no matter what.

He stood to meet them. "Hi," he said. "I wish I could tell you what's happening, but…"

Killian nodded, breathless. "I just talked to the pediatrician on my cell. They're doing a C-section. The first baby's in the wrong position."

"So many babies today are delivered by C-section," Chloe said, patting Killian's arm. "We'll find a nurse. They'll take you back to her—"

The veteran nurse appeared in the doorway at that very moment. "Mr. Abbott," she said, smiling at Killian, "I saw the limo pull up. Come on. We'll get you gowned. She's doing just fine."

Killian followed her, and Chloe sat down beside Brian. "Having built the hospital does afford you special treatment," she said. "How did you find Cordie?"

He explained his foray into Hudson River Ice Cream, and Cordie's trip to the bathroom and the startling news on her return about "fingers."

"Mon Dieu!" she exclaimed. "Are you sure the babies are all right?"

"Well, I spoke to the doctor through the nine-one-one operator and he said the babies would be okay as long as she didn't push and we hurried. I kept in touch with them all the way, and they sent a police car to lead us the rest of the way through traffic."

Chloe's face softened and she wrapped him in a fragrant embrace. "Thank you, Brian," she said.

"All I did was drive."

"You might have saved my grandchildren."

Daniel picked up the contents of the chair on the

other side of Brian and sat down, holding them in his lap. "You certainly saved *me* from having a stroke," he said. "I don't do well with women in labor. Kezia threw me out of the room every time she delivered." Suddenly realizing what he held, he studied them. "This purse doesn't go with what you're wearing, Mr. Brian," he said with a straight face. "And what did you go and buy at—" he held up the bag to read the name emblazoned on the front "—Midnight Lingerie?"

"Some blue-lace stuff," Brian returned, relieved enough to have reinforcements that he could joke. "I'm saving it for formal occasions."

Chloe hugged him again. "Have you had your lunch?"

"Ah…" He thought once more of his mocha and ice cream, in a puddle on the floor of the rental car. He would have to pay a cleaning penalty for sure. "No, I haven't." He glanced up at the clock. It was almost one in the afternoon.

"I'll go to the cafeteria," she said, "and bring something back. You wait for Janet."

"No." He pulled gently on her arm when she tried to stand. "I'll go. You wait here for news." He had to know. "Where is Janet?"

"Kezia was off to a doctor's appointment and Janet was helping Grace, Eddie and Emma finish up a batch of cookies when your call came. She'll be along as soon as Kezia gets home to stay with the children."

So that was it. "What would you like to eat?"

"A salad. Or a sandwich—turkey. And tea, please."

"Okay, coming up. Anything for you, Daniel?"

"Coffee would be good, thank you, Mr. Brian."

"Sure thing. Be right back."

Brian made his way to the cafeteria, happy to have something to do. He wondered if Janet had told Chloe and Killian what she'd discovered about her aunt. Chloe hadn't mentioned it, but then her focus, understandably, had been on Cordie and the babies.

He also wondered if Janet had given her mother and brother an earful about him. Chloe hadn't treated him any differently from the way she always did, but again, her mind had been on other things. The noble thing would be to explain to Chloe himself why he'd made the decision to leave—that he loved her daughter more than anything, and her sons, as well—but tonight wasn't the time to bring up the subject.

He made a mental picture of Killian and Cordie at home with two healthy babies, and prayed that creating the image would make it so.

The cafeteria was empty of everyone but a young woman behind the counter in hairnet and food-service gloves. She produced two turkey sandwiches in a sack, a carry box with three paper cups in it, then pointed him to the coffeemaker and hot water carafe against the wall.

As he went to get drinks, he noticed a figure seated in the farthest corner of the last table, staring at a soda can, completely oblivious to his presence. It was Joe Fanelli. He looked tired, sad and friendless.

Brian changed direction, put his tray down on the table and took a chair opposite him. "Hi, Joe," he said. "What are you doing here?"

Joe seemed to have to force his attention away from the can to look at him. Then his miserable expression worsened.

"You're home." He gave the impression that wasn't good news. Then he added quickly, "Don't worry about the shop. My mother's covering for me. She works for my grandfather all the time, so she knows how to run a cash—"

Brain raised a hand to stop the explanation. "I came to see what's wrong with you. Why are you here?"

He firmed his lips, then explained in a raspy voice, "Natty lost the baby."

Brian reached across the table to put a hand to his arm. He remembered how certain Joe had been that he could meet the challenges of fatherhood. Obviously he felt the loss deeply. "Joe, I'm sorry."

Joe nodded, gulped an unsteady breath, then cleared his throat. "Thanks. Natty called me early this morning and I brought her to the E.R. She can't stop crying. They gave her something to relax her and she finally fell asleep." He glanced at his watch. "She should be up pretty soon. Then I can take her home."

"I'm sorry," Brian said again. "They say everything happens for a purpose, but it's really hard to figure out what that is, sometimes."

"Her parents think this means I'm out of her life now, but I'm not." He pushed the soda can away and sat up. "I want to stay and help her get over the baby. I mean…I know she won't get over it, but I can help her adjust to it. I want to keep my job, if that's okay with you, until next term. Then I'm going to go to school and learn to run a business. I've learned a lot from my grandfather, and I've already picked up stuff watching you." He drew a steadier breath and even sat a little taller. "I'm going to have a Fortune 500 company someday. Then her parents will change their minds about me. Now they think I'm just the jerk who got her pregnant. But when she was scared and needed somebody, she called *me*. When somebody loves you like that, it's a responsibility, and I know that. I really, really wanted the baby, and I was going to do the absolute best I could to make her happy."

Brian nodded, sure that was true.

"But now I can prove that I'm responsible. I'm going to study hard, and work hard, and be so good to her and for her that they'll *have* to change their minds about me. Will you let me work for you holidays and summers?"

"Absolutely. And if everything's in good shape when I go back to the shop, we'll talk about the raise."

"Thanks." Joe reached across the table to shake Brian's hand, then he glanced at his watch again and stood. "I'd better go back and see if she's awake. She's brokenhearted, but I have a lot of hopeful things to tell her—later, when she's ready."

The boy's eyes were filled with emotion, and Brian found himself having to clear his own throat, as well. "Good luck, Joe. Take a couple of days off to be with Natty."

"Thanks, Brian."

Brian poured two coffees and a tea, and thought that that was a good lesson in taking charge of a bad situation. The kid would go far. He hoped Natty deserved him.

Brian walked out of the cafeteria with his purchases and came face-to-face with Janet.

Chapter Fourteen

Janet stood toe-to-toe with Brian and experienced a surge of love so strong it defeated her intention to punch him in the nose. But she was still so angry at him she could have done it anyway.

And she saw love in his eyes; she knew she did. Of course, his love for her wasn't in question. It was his unwillingness to give it to her for a lifetime because of some misguided belief that association with him would hurt her and her family.

"Good afternoon, Elliott," she said pleasantly, stepping around him to go into the cafeteria.

She was at the counter, paying for a brownie, when he appeared at her side. She should just have coffee, but she wasn't going to get through restoring her future and waiting for word of Cordie and Killian's babies without chocolate.

"Elliott?" he asked.

"Yes, I know you're Elliott," she said, switching her cup to the arm that held her purse and offering him her hand. "I'm Millicent Fortesque."

He ignored her hand. He appeared to be on his last nerve. She could just imagine how horrifying the rush to the hospital with Cordie must have been for him.

"Janet, what are you doing?" he asked.

She withdrew her hand, put her cup under the "Regular" coffee spigot. She glanced at him over her shoulder. "You're denying who you are. I want to play, too. Can't we *both* be somebody else?"

"Watch the cup!" he warned, and she spun quickly to turn off the spigot before the hot coffee burned her.

He shifted his weight. "What are you talking about?"

Keeping up a strong head of anger was difficult when her heart twisted at the sight of him. When somewhere under his annoyance with her, love was visible.

"I'm talking about your denial that you belong in the Abbott family," she said, tearing off a bite of brownie. "Your denial that you're the man who loves me."

"I never denied either of those things."

"You're leaving us. That's denial."

"Yeah," he retorted angrily. "Well, I seem to be very much here, don't I? Excuse me." He held up the sack. "I promised your mother a sandwich." And he walked off toward the waiting room.

Janet had no idea what he meant. Getting Cordie to the hospital had held him up from preparing to leave? Or he wasn't as eager to leave as he'd thought he was? She nibbled on her brownie, trying to buck herself up as she followed the corridor in the direction Brian had taken. If he was grumpy because he was confused, that was a good thing.

Chloe was eating her sandwich and explaining to Daniel what Janet and Brian had discovered about Kate when Janet returned to the waiting room. Daniel, adding creamer to his coffee, stopped to listen in disbelief when she got to the part about Bristol perpetrating the kidnapping right in front of Corbin Girard's passing car—and Corbin never saying a word.

"The bastard!" Daniel exclaimed.

Janet saw Brian's slight start, as though he'd been poked with a stick. Then she watched her mother and the chauffeur continue to talk about Corbin's part in the story and realized they weren't being insensitive to him. They simply didn't consider him involved. No one blamed him.

Brian looked at her as she sat opposite him and she gave him a "So there!" tip of her head.

"Any news from the delivery room?" Janet asked.

"Nothing yet," her mother replied.

A long two hours followed, during which they all talked about nothing, flipped through magazines, went for more coffee and tea.

Then Killian, in gown and mask, walked into the waiting room. He pulled off the mask and said with a bright smile, "They're going to be fine. They'll need help breathing for a couple of weeks. But, except for weak lung development from being early, they're healthy."

Chloe stood to hug him. "I knew it, I knew it! How's Cordie?"

"Still sleeping from the surgery, but she'll be fine, too."

Janet went to be part of the hug, then Daniel was embraced.

Brian stood in line to shake Killian's hand, but Killian wrapped him in a quick, tight hug, instead. "I hate to think of what could have happened if you hadn't been there, Brian."

"As I keep saying," Brian insisted, "all I did was drive."

"The doctor said your speed in getting her here saved them." The emotion in Killian's eyes was intense against his pallor. "Now you've given me back my brother, my children, possibly even my wife." He hugged him more tightly. "There's no damage your father could have done that would top that."

"Killian…"

"Even passively helping Bristol get away with Janby. We have her back and you helped her solve the mystery. The only thing that'll get you in trouble with any of us is if you don't make her happy."

A hard lump formed in Janet's throat. Killian always knew how things were—though he might be mistaken this time. A figure suddenly appeared in the doorway of the office across the hall and a camera flash blinded them all before they could even react.

But Janet heard Brian's quiet oath and the sound of footsteps racing down the corridor.

Daniel tried to follow, but Janet pushed him back toward her mother, blinking to clear her eyes. "Let me go. I'm probably the only one who can save the reporter's life.

"Save it?" she heard Daniel say as she took off after Brian. "That wasn't my plan!"

As she rounded the corner, she saw Brian with a fistful of Merriman's jacket, pushing him out the side door. She hurried to catch up and found them outdoors in the busy parking lot. Brian dragged him toward an empty, grassy area behind the hospital. Certain he intended bodily harm, she added speed to her pursuit.

"Brian!" she shouted. He now had the reporter by the shirtfront and had slammed him up against the back wall.

He didn't hear her. Buzz's camera was in Brian's free hand and she didn't want to think about what he was going to do with it.

"Bri-an!" She reached his side, breathing heavily. "Please don't. He's not…"

But Brian still wasn't listening. Buzz was half a head shorter than he was and looked scared, despite a frail attempt at bravado.

"I have my Fifth Amendment rights!" he said a little shakily. "I can…"

Brian pushed harder with the hand that held the shirt, the knuckles of his fist applying pressure to Buzz's trachea. "If you don't stop harassing this woman," he said in a tone of voice she'd never heard before, "the only right you'll have is that of choosing the color of the receptacle that will hold your broken body."

"She's news! She—"

"She's a woman!" Brian roared back at him. "Not some lifeless thing you can chase around for your own enjoyment."

Buzz struggled against him, and Brian leaned into his

grip, his blue eyes dark and dangerous. "If I see a photo of her sitting in the hospital waiting room, you're dead, do you understand me?"

The reporter hesitated.

"Or do I have to use your camera as an example of what will happen to you?" He held it up as though intending to slam it against the wall.

"No! I'll get you for destruction of property!"

"You're not hearing me." Brian took aim.

"All right! All right!" Buzz choked a little and pulled at Brian's hand. "No...pictures. I...promise."

"Ever again."

"Oh, com—"

"*Ever* again."

"Okay, okay. No pictures. Ever...again."

"Good." Brian freed him and he slumped against the wall with a little cry of relief. Brian pushed the camera at his midsection and he took it. "I want the film you just took."

Buzz didn't even quibble. He opened the back, removed the film, handed it over.

"Now," Brian said, and smiled amiably, "if you want to write about me, do your worst. I don't care. There's enough sordid stuff in my life to keep you going indefinitely. And more coming all the time." Then his tone and his expression darkened. "But if I read one more word about the Abbotts, or see one photograph..."

"I know." Buzz put a hand over one ear, clearly unwilling to listen to the consequences again. "I heard you."

"All right, then. Get out of here."

Buzz needed a minute to regain his coordination, but the moment he did, he ran off toward his truck.

Brian directed his attention to Janet. This man, free of civilizing influences and the caution she'd come to know and rail against, made her realize she'd finally pushed him too far. He'd abandoned familiar behavior to get rid of the things in his life that were plaguing him. She realized grimly that she was probably next.

"And you..." he said, taking her shirtfront in a fist and pulling her to him.

BRIAN LOOKED DOWN into Janet's upturned face, her dark eyes uncertain and worried, and thought with a burning in his throat how close he'd come to losing all the light she'd brought into his life.

Until he'd heard a kid almost half his age explain to him that having someone love you was a responsibility you couldn't walk away from.

Until Killian Abbott had told him with absolute sincerity that whatever Brian's father had done would never stand up to the lives Brian had restored to him. Overstated, certainly, but nice to hear. And just a few hours of imagining his life without Janet in it made him willing to believe it.

He kissed her in apology for all the emotion he'd withheld to simplify a goodbye, Then again with the promise of all the myriad ways in which he intended to make it up to her.

"I owe you a three-carat diamond," he said when he

raised his head, "and a long, delicious honeymoon somewhere."

She stared at him in stupefaction. "How...come?"

"Remember when I told you I would never go near an altar and you challenged that by asking me if I was a betting man?"

She smiled cautiously. "Yeah?"

"Well, you won. You could find me near an altar any day you choose."

Her smile widened and gained confidence. "Is that a proposal?"

"It's the last gasp of a dying man," he said, kissing her again. "If you don't agree to marry me, I'm done for."

"Yes." She kissed him back.

"Yes, I'm done for—or yes, you'll marry me?"

"Yes, I'll marry you."

Thank God. But he was probably done for anyway.

Epilogue

The second week in October the Duchess's crop matured from leaf-green to light greenish-yellow. The honeymooning couples were home, and everyone gathered around Campbell as he climbed a ladder placed against the largest tree in the Vintage part of the orchard. They watched anxiously while he took an apple in hand, turned it up, then opened his fingers to show that it had released. It was time to pick.

Now, the fourth week in October, there were apples everywhere—in boxes on the ground, in trucks going to and from the wholesaler in Milton, NY, and fruit that was less than perfect was all over the kitchen counter, on the dining room table and in boxes on the kitchen floor, awaiting Kezia's sauce, pies, brown Betty.

The harvest would go on for another several weeks and include the major part of the orchard. The work was hard and everyone was exhausted. Even Brian had employed Joe full-time at the store so that he could help the family pick.

The priest from St. Paul's had come to the orchard

one evening a week ago and married Janby and Brian among the apple trees, surrounded by their family and friends. Even six-week-old Brian and Abigail Abbott, finally home from the hospital, had been able to attend.

Brian had tried to talk Killian and Cordie out of naming their son after him. "I understand naming the little girl Abigail. It's a longstanding family name. But Brian…"

Killian had put the little boy in his arms. "Brian is a new family name. Here. Hold him."

And Brian had stopped protesting.

Janet was sure every bride remembered the details of her wedding day, but she wondered if any other bride had ever had the sensory banquet she and Brian had enjoyed. The air had been heavy with the smell of apples, and the wood smoke and salt that were so familiar on Long Island.

She'd asked everyone to dress comfortably for an outdoor wedding in October, and the sight of them had been a feast for the eye—woolens and weaves in gold, red and forest-green against the autumn mist weaving through the apple-heavy orchard. And they'd all looked so happy.

She remembered Brian's firm and steady voice promising to love her forever, and her own vows to do the same. She'd felt so warm, so loved.

They'd been sleeping in his room at Shepherd's Knoll during the harvest, and a week in his arms had made her forget all the difficulties they'd endured to come together. Her life felt so big, and she was so focused on the moment, that whatever sadness she'd known was forgotten.

Now they all sat on the porch at sunset on a Friday afternoon to celebrate the week's hard work. In deference to the change of season, Kezia had substituted her famous peach martinis with spiked apple cider for the adults and plain apple cider for Sophie and Sawyer's children.

Chloe raised her glass to the already darkening sky. "I wish to toast the generosity of God in heaven."

Janet saw her brothers look at one another doubtfully.

"Maman," Campbell said. He was seated beside China on an Adirondack love seat, his arm around her shoulders. "Lightning might smite us. I'm not sure it's right to toast God, particularly with alcohol."

Chloe shook her head. "This is not just alcohol. This was made from our apples. We're toasting God with the fruits of our labors—literally. And He is prayed to all the time. I'm sure He enjoys being toasted—proof that we honor Him in our number."

Killian, a twin in one arm and Cordie, holding the other twin, in his other arm, released Cordie to raise his glass. "Okay. I'm with you. What are we toasting?"

"The fact that less than a year ago, we were one lonely woman, a pair of faithful friends…" She raised her glass to Kezia and Daniel, who sat together on a bench near the railing, glasses in hand. "And three men who were…lost."

Each Abbott first seemed to resist that description, then decide it was right.

"And now…" Chloe looked around at the brood that had become a crowd. Sophie, Sawyer and their three children took up the rest of the bench along one side of the porch. "Look at us. My boys are happy, we have children and babies, and…" She turned to Janet and Brian, sitting together in a deck chair. "Abby's home, and she's found her personal home with the son I claim from Susannah."

She raised her glass to heaven. Everyone stood and did the same. "Thank you, God," she said. "Bless our harvest, bless our family—those we've lost…" She smiled at the sky. "We still love you, Nathan. Those who came before us and those who come after us. Bless forever the love that brings us together and holds us in a common heart."

They drank, watched the sun set, then went inside together.

Welcome to the world of American Romance! Turn the page for excerpts from our October 2005 titles.

THE LATE BLOOMER'S BABY by Kaitlyn Rice
SAVING JOE by Laura Marie Altom
THE SECRET WEDDING DRESS by Roz Denny Fox
A FABULOUS HUSBAND by Dianne Castell

We hope you'll enjoy every one of these books!

*Kaitlyn Rice knows the heartland of the
country—she herself lives in Kansas.
This is her first story in a miniseries entitled
HEARTLAND SISTERS, about the Blume girls,
Callie, Isabel and Josie. In this story,
Callie's estranged husband, Ethan, shows up
and is completely unaware that the little boy who
goes everywhere with her is his.
Callie has no plans to share her secret
with the man who once abandoned her.
So why can't she sign those divorce papers
releasing him—and her—from their vows?*

Available October 2005

"Let's have a look, Miz Blume." The disaster worker's eyes met Callie's briefly before sinking to the stack of papers she'd just handed him.

She wasn't a Blume anymore. Callie frowned, but didn't bother to correct him. The man appeared to be around her age, twenty-nine, so he must remember her from her childhood here in Augusta, Kansas. That would explain the vague familiarity of his features, as well as the dull greeting he'd offered when she'd sat down across the table from him.

Local folks would probably always think of Callie as one of the Blume girls, and that was fine. Although she signed legal documents as Calliope Taylor now, she hadn't really considered herself a married woman for almost two years. Not since the day Ethan had abandoned her—and their marriage.

As she often did when she thought about her husband, Callie ran her thumb over the back of her wedding band. These days, she wore the ring mostly for convenience. If she didn't have an irresistibly cute, diaper-clad reason to shy away from legal proceedings, Callie would mail the band to Ethan, divorce him and reclaim her maiden name.

But she didn't want to rekindle her husband's interest in her life. He didn't know about the baby. Thanks to a miracle of science, he had actually left before Callie was pregnant.

A spiraling complexity of fertility treatments had failed during the previous twenty-six cycles, so Callie had held little hope for that last set of appointments at the clinic. And, after all, her husband had left her six weeks before.

She had imagined how wonderful life would be if Ethan came home to such happy news, and she'd kept up with every shot and blood test and ultrasound. Miraculously, the procedure had worked—but Ethan had never returned.

Callie hadn't been able to surrender her broken heart to seek him out and tell him. She'd been alone when she made the decision to try one last time. She'd been alone when she nurtured herself through pregnancy and childbirth. She'd gone on with her life. The precious eleven-month-old boy was hers alone.

Welcome to the first book in Laura Marie Altom's
U.S. MARSHALS miniseries.
There are four siblings in the Logue family—
and they've all become marshals. Gillian is
the only girl, however, and she sometimes
wonders whether she's cut out for the job,
or whether she should be the traditional woman
she thinks her brothers want her to be.
This story takes place on a small island
off the coast of Oregon—and with Laura's
wonderful descriptions, you can almost
smell the ocean!

Available October 2005

"Mr. Morgan?" Gillian Logue called above the driving rain.

The man she sought just stood there at the grumbling surf's edge, staring at an angry North Pacific, his expression far more treacherous than any storm. Hands tucked deep in his pockets, broad shoulders braced against the wind, he didn't even look real—more like some mythical sea king surveying all that was rightfully his.

What had him so deep in thought that he hadn't noticed Gillian approach? Two years had passed since his wife's death. Surely by now he'd let his anger go?

Gillian shivered, hunching deeper into her pathetic excuse for a jacket. Even in the rain, the place reeked of fish and seaweed, and all things foreign to her L.A. beat. They were achingly familiar smells, and she could try all she liked to pretend they didn't dredge up matters best left in the past, but there was no denying it—she had issues with coming home to Oregon. Not that this island was home, but the boulder-strewn coastal landscape sure was.

The crashing waves.

The tangy scent of pines flavored with a rich stew of all things living and dead in the sea.

The times she'd played along the shore as a child.

The times she'd cried along the shore as a woman.

Shoot, who was she to judge Joe?

She wasn't on this godforsaken rock to make a new friend. She was here for one simple reason—to do her job. "Mr. Morgan?" she called again.

He shot a look over his shoulder and narrowed his eyes, not bothering to shield them from the rain. "Yeah," he finally shouted. "That's me. Who are you? What do you want?"

The stiff breeze whipped strands of her blondish hair around her face and she took a second to brush them away before stepping close enough to hold out her hand. "Hi," she said. "I'm U.S. Marshal Gillian Logue." Flipping open a black leather wallet, she flashed him her silver star.

"I asked you a question," he said.

"I heard you." She lifted her chin a fraction higher, hoping the slight movement conveyed at least a dozen messages, the loudest of which was that she might be housed in a small, pretty package, but she considered herself tough as any man—especially him. "I'm here on official business. Over a year ago, the drug lord responsible for killing your wife was released on a technicality. Now we have him back and we'd like you to testify."

The man she'd studied quite literally for months eyed her long and hard, delivered a lifeless laugh of his own then turned his back on her and headed down the beach for the trail leading to his cabin.

"Like it or not, Mr. Morgan, I'm staying!"

*Roz Denny Fox, who also writes for
Superromance and Harlequin's new
Signature imprint, is known for the warmth
and realness of her characters and the charm
of her writing. Her first American Romance,
Too Many Brothers, was published last year,
and now we're delighted to present
The Secret Wedding Dress. It, too, is an
IN THE FAMILY story. Roz strongly believes
in the importance of family and community,
which is reflected in both of these books.
So is her irrepressible sense of humor.
You'll smile and laugh when you read
this book—and you'll feel good.*

Available October 2005

Through an open window in her sewing room, Sylvie Shea heard car doors slamming, followed by men's voices, and very briefly, the voice of a child. She was seated on the floor, busily stitching a final row of seed pearls around the hem of an ivory satin wedding dress, but the commotion outside enticed her to abandon her project. Her rustic log cabin nestled into the base of the Great Smoky Mountains didn't exactly sit on a high volume traffic street—nor did any street in her sleepy hamlet of Briarwood, North Carolina. But as her family reminded her often enough, a woman living alone on the fringe of a forest couldn't be too careful. She'd better spare a moment to investigate.

Pushing aside the dress form that held the cream-colored gown, she squeezed her way through six other forms displaying finished bridesmaids' dresses for her good friend Kay Waller's upcoming nuptials.

A tenth headless mannequin stood in a corner. Sylvie automatically straightened the opaque sheet covering *that* dress, making sure the gown remained hidden from prying eyes. Satisfied the cover was secure, she walked to the oversized picture window she'd had installed in what once served as Bill and Mary Shea's sunporch.

The shouts hadn't abated, and Sylvie parted the curtain she'd sewn from mantilla lace. The filmy weave gave her plenty of light to sew, yet didn't fade any of the fine fabrics stored on bolts along a side wall. Removing the lace filter, a bright shaft of July sun momentarily blinded her.

Blinking several times, at first she couldn't see any reason for the racket. Then as she pressed her nose flat to the sun-kissed glass, Sylvie noticed a large moving van parked in the lane next door.

Iva Whitaker's home had been closed up over a year. At times, Sylvie all but forgot there was a structure beyond her wild-rose covered fence. Iva's land shared a border with Sylvie's, and included a lake fed by a stream running through Sylvie's wooded lot. She often wondered why, when both the Whitakers and the Sheas had owned five acres, they'd built their homes within spitting distance of each other. Iva, though, had been a dear neighbor. If Sylvie was to have new ones, as the moving truck would indicate, she hoped the same could be said of them.

After a moment, she saw a man with straight, honey-blond hair appear, unloading a small pet carrier from a dusty white, seven-passenger van parked to the right of the moving van. He looked thirtyish, was about medium height, and had a wiry build. His only real distinguishing feature was gold, wire-rimmed glasses. Sylvie saw him as sort of a corporate version of country singer Keith Urban.

The man set out several suitcases, slammed the hatch and disappeared behind a thicket of colorful sweet peas. Sylvie was left searching her memory bank for particulars of Iva's will. If she'd heard anything said about relatives, she'd forgotten the specifics.

Sylvie made a point of avoiding gossip, the occupational pastime of too many in Briarwood. Five years ago *she'd* been the prime topic. Sylvie doubted a soul among the town's 3,090 residents gave a second thought to how badly the rumors had hurt. Certainly everyone in town was well aware that becoming a top New York City wedding gown designer had been Sylvie's lifelong dream. Her best friends and their parents were privy to the fact she imagined prospective brides coveting a Sylvie Shea gown with the same reverence the rich and famous spoke the name of Vera Wang.

So it'd shocked her that people whispered about her—when at twenty-one, she abruptly left New York and returned home to live in the hand-hewn structure she'd inherited from her father's parents. They must have seen her distress over murmurs claiming she'd left Briarwood at eighteen with stars in her eyes and magic in her fingers, only to return at twenty-one with teary eyes and a heart in tatters.

Broken by a man. Or so gossips speculated then and now. What really happened in New York would remain her humiliating secret.

*Come back to Whistler's Bend, Montana,
in this second book of Dianne Castell's humorous
miniseries FORTY & FABULOUS.
Dr. Barbara Jean Fairmont and Colonel
Flynn MacIntire have never gotten along,
but now she needs a favor from him.
B.J. wants a baby, but the trouble is,
she's forty, and husbandless, and qualifying for
adoption is tough. She has an idea for a perfect
arrangement...or does she?*

Available October 2005

Dr. Barbara Jean Fairmont peered across the Cut Loose Saloon to Colonel Flynn MacIntire, the guy who'd ran her panties up the high school flagpole, read her diary over the loudspeaker and called her brainiac. Even if that had happened twenty-two years ago, some things a woman never forgot.

Of course, she also couldn't forget the oatmeal she'd put in his football helmet or her article about jocks running up and down the field because they were lost.

Fairmont and MacIntire, the Brain and the Brawn. They had nothing in common and managed to avoid each other…until now. He was on leave from the army with an injured leg and his grandmother had asked B.J. to help him. He hadn't taken her calls, so tracking him to the saloon was a last-ditch effort.

A country-and-Western singer warbled from the jukebox as B.J. snaked her way through sparsely populated tables and a lung-clogging haze of smoke. Flynn sat alone, cigarette in hand, table littered with longnecks, not doing himself one bit of good. "If you quit swilling beer and puffing cancer sticks, agree to get off your butt and do therapy, maybe I can help you."

He looked up, and she gave his two-day beard, wrinkled clothes and incredible ocean-blue eyes a once-over and shuddered. Because of his appearance or because of those eyes?

Unfortunately, because of his eyes…and broad shoulders, and muscled arms and all the other delicious body parts that had driven her secretly insane for as long as she could remember. Usually, her irrational attraction to the man wasn't a problem because Flynn was not around for her to obsess over. But, oh Lordy, he was here now and likely to stay unless he got better and went back to his army life.

He leaned back and folded his arms across his solid broad chest. His index finger on his left hand was slightly crooked, as if it had been broken and not set properly; he had a thick scar on his neck, a wider new one on his chin line, and a he was graying at the temples. A soldier. A *fighting* soldier, who'd seen more than his share of combat. She could only imagine what he'd been through and she hated it. But he'd returned alive, and that was something to be hugely thankful for, *though she wished he'd returned somewhere else.*

HARLEQUIN®

AMERICAN *Romance*®

★ US MARSHALS
BORN AND BRED

Introducing the first in a four-book series
about a family of U.S. Marshals by

Laura Marie Altom

SAVING JOE

(#1086, October 2005)

Gillian Logue's first assignment as a U.S. Marshal takes her to the beautiful Oregon coast of her youth, and into the path of the widower Joe Morgan. It's her job to keep him safe, but he claims he doesn't want her kind of help. When Gillian tries to convince him that his little girl needs him, it's only a matter of time before Joe starts seeing Gillian as more than a law-enforcement officer, and begins to recognize that maybe she can save him in more ways than one....

Watch for the next book in the series,
coming in January 2006!

Available wherever Harlequin books are sold.

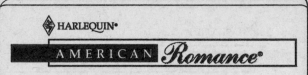

40 & Fabulous

Dianne Castell

presents three very funny books about
three women who have grown up together in
Whistler's Bend, Montana. These friends are
turning forty and are struggling to deal with it.
But who said you can't be forty and fabulous?

A FABULOUS HUSBAND

(#1088, October 2005)

Dr. BJ Fairmont wants a baby, but being forty and
single, her hopes for adoption are fading fast. Until
Colonel Flynn MacIntire proposes that she nurse him
back to active duty in exchange for a marriage
certificate, that is. Is the town's fabulous bachelor
really the answer to her prayers?

Also look for:

A FABULOUS WIFE

(#1077, August 2005)

A FABULOUS WEDDING

(#1095, December 2005)

Available wherever Harlequin books are sold.

e♦HARLEQUIN.com

The Ultimate Destination for Women's Fiction

The ultimate destination for women's fiction.
Visit eHarlequin.com today!

GREAT BOOKS:
- We've got something for everyone—and at great low prices!
- Choose from new releases, backlist favorites, Themed Collections and preview upcoming books, too.
- Favorite authors: Debbie Macomber, Diana Palmer, Susan Wiggs and more!

EASY SHOPPING:
- Choose our convenient "bill me" option. No credit card required!
- Easy, secure, 24-hour shopping from the comfort of your own home.
- Sign-up for free membership and get $4 off your first purchase.
- Exclusive online offers: FREE books, bargain outlet savings, hot deals.

EXCLUSIVE FEATURES:
- Try Book Matcher—finding your favorite read has never been easier!
- Save & redeem Bonus Bucks.
- Another reason to love Fridays— Free Book Fridays!

─── Shop online ───
at www.eHarlequin.com today!

INTBB204R